The Final Word

An Agent Orion Adventure

CODY GOGGIN

Table of Contents

Chapter One

The brass handle had been stained with blood. Everything else on the way had appeared perfectly natural and untouched. But in an unusual showing of carelessness, the thief had left behind a surefire sign that he had been there. Agent Orion, or Jon Burrows to those who knew him more personally, reached for the handle with caution.

Only seven hours earlier he had been on a plane flying from Arcadia to Tesaline. It was beautiful rainforest country, but Jon found the heat annoying. The smell of sweat never seemed to waver as he had made his way from the small airport through the shambling village.

The only high rise building in sight had been his destination. An apartment complex for those more fortunate than the common people on the island. Rich folk with dirty agendas.

But now he found himself at the top floor and knowing he was too late before he even entered the room. The doorknob turned with a slip between his fingers that left them red. Inside, the scene was astonishingly quiet. No furniture had been moved, nothing disheveled, all but for the gurgling dying man at the center of the floor.

Jon rushed to his side and examined him for open wounds or signs of trauma. It was too late. Likely, he had been fed some form of suicide capsule. His breathing was growing ever more strained by the moment.

"Who did this to you?" asked Jon. "Why did they do this to you?" But the man struggled to find his voice.

Jon grabbed the man by the back of the head and tilted him forward to get more air.

"*Ruby*." was all he managed to say before slipping into the abyss.

Jon found himself standing in a room with a dead man with little to go on next. The killer would surely be long gone, nothing appeared to have been messed with in the apartment, and the dead man had provided no explanation. Given that agents were not generally given the names of their clients, Jon also knew very little about why he had been summoned here in the first place.

"Sorry chap," he said. With a nod and a bound to the door, he was gone again.

As the white sports car he'd been given to travel with during his stay in Tesaline glided over the asphalt road leading to his hotel, Jon pondered. It would be easy enough to relay the information on what had happened to his superior and move on to another case. But he felt that there was more to this that needed getting to the bottom of. The phone call to S.O. would be a difficult one tonight.

Seeing no sense in rushing into something like that, Jon decided to stop off for a visit to examine the nightlife. The long drive from village to city had left him thirsty.

Casino after casino with the usual flare were decorated with gaudy lights that poured out into the night sky. Hustlers and corner girls lined the sidewalk looking for their chance to make an income. The city was Barley, and it was known for its share of depravity and corruption.

But here on the street level people generally looked happy. The party atmosphere stretched from face to face as people swayed to music coming from musicians hoping to be noticed.

Jon drove his car to the end of the strip and turned around. The first establishment on the right would do him for the evening. The valet took his key and Jon eyed over his shoulder as the sports car faded away to parts unknown. When he turned around there was a girl directly in front of him.

"You look lonely tonight mister," she said, grazing her hand along his chest.

"Lucky for me there are so many people here to keep me company," said Jon.

"A crowd isn't company. We could find someplace private," said the girl.

"I'm afraid not. Shouldn't you have school tomorrow?" Jon smiled at the girl. She wasn't much younger than he was, but she was too young to be here. "There are finer ways to make money, I assure you. You deserve better."

She cussed him as he walked away but Jon paid her no mind. The lights and the sounds of the casino beckoned him through the door and away he went.

"Hello sir," said a small man with a too-tight tuxedo. "Welcome to The Bliss, where your dreams can and will come true."

"Thank you," said Jon. "Can you point me to the blackjack table?"

The host pointed a wiry finger toward a series of tables serving up blackjack in spades. "That way. But perhaps you'd like a drink first?"

"Of course," said Jon.

"Then you can place an order with any of our floor girls. They're the one's with the silver dresses. Can't miss them."

Jon glanced around the entire room full of slot machines and poker tables and saw three women going around serving drinks and taking orders. He tipped the small man a few dollars.

"Thank you," he said.

Jon sifted through people as they passed along in various states of joy and disappointment. Some were clutching pouches full of coins and others held their sacks limply by their side, empty. The casino smelled of cigarette smoke and booze mixed with too much perfume. At least it didn't smell like sweat. Truthfully, Jon loved the smell.

"Excuse me," he said, as he approached the woman in the silver dress.

"What can I get you honey?" said the woman.

"Rum and seltzer, if you would," said Jon. "Say, what can you tell me about this place?"

"The pay is no good and the slots don't win," she said with a laugh. "But you didn't hear it from me."

"That's alright. I'm a blackjack man."

"Of course, you are," said the server, as she shimmied away to produce Jon's drink.

The blackjack table with the least amount of people surrounding it was Jon's first pick. The dealer behind the cards was a large man with a dirty mustache. His gray hair betrayed his physical stature. At one time he was probably a fantastic bouncer for the casino.

"Wassup, bub?" he asked Jon.

"I was looking to get in on the action."

The woman who had been playing for a while stepped aside to make room for Jon at the table. Her brown hair hung loosely around her neck, and she was far too stunning to be hanging around a place like The Bliss. The black dress she wore clung to her flowing hips, and she moved with an unusual grace.

"You're staring," she said with an accent that Jon didn't recognize.

"It seems I've gone temporarily blind," said Jon.

"Is that so? Is the view that bad?" she asked.

"It's as bright as the sun, you see," said Jon with a twist of his lips.

The woman shook her head, and the dealer did his best to interrupt. "Are yuns' here to play cards er' what?"

The dealer gave them their hand and Jon leaned to peak at his overturned card. An eight was his hidden card to pair with the seven that everyone could see.

The dealer held a nine and the woman was left with a five. Jon turned to her as she put her overturned card back to the table.

"Any luck?" he asked.

"I guess you've never played poker before?" she joked.

"I'm not good at keeping secrets," said Jon.

The woman laughed. "Somehow, I bet you are." She shook her head. "All men are."

"Okay, we're playin' blackjack 'ere," said the dealer. "Get on with it."

"Hit me," said the woman.

"You play rough?" asked Jon.

"Excuse me?"

"What's your name?" asked Jon.

The dealer passed the woman her card. It was a ten, and she seemed pleased by this. "My name is Sheena. You don't need to know my last name."

"I'll tell you mine if you tell me yours," said Jon with the wink of an eye.

Sheena leaned her head back and laughed earnestly. "You are something else. I'll give you that much."

The dealer grabbed Jon by the shoulder and shook him. "What will it be bub?

"Right, hit me."

"I just might," said Sheena.

The five card Jon needed skipped across the table and he stopped it with an outstretched finger. The dealer then drew a card for himself.

"I've busted," said the dealer.

"I've got twenty," said Sheena as she flipped her cards over for the others to see.

Jon eyed his overturned card and smiled at having twenty-one. But he merely slipped the card back upside down. "I've busted as well."

Sheena cocked her head to the side, and she gave Jon a once over. "Who are you?" she asked.

"Jon. But you don't need to know my last name," he jested.

"Maybe not, but I do need to know more." Sheena took the coins from the table and slipped them into a small bag. "Will you join me for a drink?"

As if destiny had intervened, the woman in the silver dress arrived with both of their drinks ready. "One vodka water and one rum seltzer," she said.

Jon took both drinks from the tray and thanked the woman. He handed the vodka over to Sheena and together they walked away from the blackjack table. She sipped her drink softly while he quickly downed the entirety of his own.

"Are you staying here?" she asked him.

"I'm afraid not. I have a room at The Wizard," said Jon.

She nearly spat her drink out. "The Wizard? And you're afraid that you don't have a room here? The Wizard is the nicest hotel in the city."

"Is it?" said Jon, honestly clueless. "I had no idea."

"You must be new here. Everyone knows this."

Jon watched as she walked through the room and the lights seemed to dance across her face with patterns that accentuated the beauty of her features. He was quite smitten.

"You're not bad looking either," she said, as she turned his head away gently with her left hand. "I like a man with dark hair."

Jon laughed as he looked down at his suit and tie. "I'm glad."

But then he noticed the blood that was still staining his hand. Jon quickly plunged it into his pocket and began to speak.

"So do you live around here?" he asked.

"At the hotel?" she responded quizzically.

"Well, the island I mean," said Jon.

"Oh, yes." she said softly.

Jon nodded along and made sure to keep his hand firmly hidden in the fabric of his pocket.

"So, can you tell me anything else about this place? Aside from The Wizard being so grand."

Sheena stopped walking and stood with her back to the golden wall that led to the elevator. "It's like any other place like this. Full of people ready to betray you at a moment's notice."

"That seems oddly specific," said Jon.

"Oh please," burst Sheena, "ask any person here and they've been betrayed by someone or something down here. You're not that naïve."

"I'm not so sure," said Jon.

"Well Jon, I want to thank you for throwing that blackjack game. I don't know why you did it, but I know the money helps."

She turned to head toward the elevator, but Jon stopped her.

"Would you like to stay at The Wizard tonight?"

Sheena looked at him suddenly with a changed expression. "Is that why you let me win that game? Some ulterior motive?"

"No, no. Of course not. Nothing like that," stammered Jon. "I just meant if you wanted to sleep somewhere nicer than this. I could take the couch."

"I don't know you and you don't know me, Jon. Thanks, but no thanks."

She kissed him on the cheek and left him standing on the casino floor with two empty drinks.

"Alright then," said Jon as the waitress drew near. "Can I have one more rum and seltzer?"

Later, as Jon arrived at The Wizard, he was amazed to see the difference. Much as Sheena had said, The Wizard was a far grander lodging place than The Bliss. The ceilings of the main hall seemed to be three floors high, and everything shone as if it had been shined that morning.

Jon avoided the casino and instead elected to check in quickly and find his room. Up the floors he went until finally he arrived at his room number and went inside.

For a moment he reflected on the day and his night. But the time was quickly arriving that he would have no choice but to call in and report what had happened in the smaller village. With great reluctance he sat himself down on the bed and reached for the telephone.

"We've been waiting for you," said the woman's voice on the other end of the line. "What took you so long?"

"Bad traffic in these parts. You should see it," said Jon.

"I know better than that. You've been out gambling and drinking again," said the woman without anger, but Jon still felt judged. "Tell us what happened."

Jon relayed the events of the day and the woman listened intently. As he finished, she thanked him and told him she'd be getting back with him for his next assignment. But he stopped her.

"Hold on. I'd like to speak to you about this one. I feel like there's more that I could do."

"That is highly irregular," said the woman's voice.

"I know but listen to me," said Jon. "I've been trying to figure out what '*Ruby*' meant all night long."

"You're not a detective, Agent Orion. It's not your place to figure these things out."

"Yes, but I want to," said Jon. "You see, I figure this guy must have been a seller of priceless jewels. Is that what got him killed? A ruby of some kind?"

The voice on the other end remained silent.

"It doesn't make sense for you to send me into these places and expect me to go in blindly. I should know more. I deserve to know more. I can be more effective for you."

Finally, she answered. "It's possible that a rare jewel may have passed through

Tesaline. We had another case that we thought was unrelated. *The Devil's Eye Ruby* has a history of getting people killed. We were tracking it, but never thought it would end up in a village like that."

"It was the man's dying word. It must be important," said Jon.

"You may be right," said the woman reluctantly. "We will get ahold of you tomorrow with more information."

"So, that's it? I'm still on the case?"

But the woman hung up and Jon's ear was greeted with the loud hum of a dial tone. "Damn," he muttered.

With a deep sigh of relief Jon removed the tie from his neck and placed it over the chair next to the bed. The jacket and slacks he hung neatly over the table by the window. Looking down from there he could see the lights and party of the city still going on without him. Somewhere in all that noise and commotion he found comfort.

Chapter Two

The next morning saw Jon making the journey back down the strip. With no destination particularly in mind he moved through the crowds to experience the scene during daylight hours. Not much was changed. People bustled about in various states of ecstasy and sadness. Some were heading to the airport for early flights off the island. Others were already heading back to the casino.

Jon grew hungry and stopped into a corner café to find breakfast. His usual order of eggs and sausage was accompanied by black coffee and fine conversation. The server there had been working on the strip for many years and had just as many stories to tell.

"I tell you, this place used to be cleaner. All gussied up and pretty. But the years go on. It's nothing like that now," he said, as Jon bit down on a forkful of eggs. "Yes, it used to be something."

"Is it mostly the same establishments along the way? Or has there been new ownership?" asked Jon.

"Oh, stuff is always changing. That place The Bliss used to be called The Highway. That is until the owner done fly from the top window."

"Good Lord, really?"

"Sure," said the man. "They say he jumped, but tell me how any man jump himself through a solid window that don't open?"

"That would be something," said Jon, intrigued.

"I figure he was murdered. Just like everyone else around here."

"What do you mean?" asked Jon.

The man behind the counter leaned back and seemed to peak around to see if anyone was listening.

"The way I figure it, about half the deaths in this city are murders. Happens all the time," said the man.

Jon shook his head. It wasn't uncommon for places like this to be the home for homicides. But the man behind the counter seemed to be referring to some grander scheme or design.

"What do you suppose is the meaning of all of it?" Jon asked.

"Money," said the man.

Jon laughed but caught himself at the sight of the serious expression on the other man's face. "Of course, money," he said.

"Well, I know that's normal. But we've had big money coming through here for a while now. Not just the casinos. *Blood money.*"

Jon finished his food and sipped his coffee.

"Kinda stuff people kill over, ya know what I'm saying? Gold and jewels and drugs," said the man behind the counter. Jon's eyebrows raised.

"Did you say jewels?" he asked the man.

"Oh, yes. Jewels, antiques, even people."

Jon nodded. "Have you ever heard of The Devil's Eye?"

The man hung his head and thought for a moment. "I can't say that I have."

Jon smiled and paid his bill. "Thank you for the conversation. Good day."

Outside a yellow sun was beating down through a perfectly blue sky. Jon barely had time to take it all in when he was bumped into by a scrawny looking young man with glasses.

"Watch it!" he began to say. But the young fellow stood up and passed Jon an envelope.

"Don't open it until you get somewhere private," said the messenger.

As he spoke, the sound of a gunshot rang out across the casino strip. Jon's eyes widened as the youth in front of him dropped to a bloody heap on the ground.

Screams echoed from every direction and people began running hysterically. Jon had little time to think before lunging into action. His .22 HDM found its way into his hands as naturally as breathing. The semi-automatic pistol felt cold against his skin as he ran for cover.

An elaborate sculpted wall became his shield as he rolled into position. From over the edge, he peered in an attempt to locate the guilty gunman. Another shot burst forth and Jon barely managed to get back behind the cover as the bullet ripped into the rock and left dust flying through the air.

Knowing he couldn't stay there, Jon crawled along the wall until he could get underneath a large truck that had been parked to deliver something. From there he was able to get back to his feet in a squatted position and move freely down the street.

Crowds of people had vanished, and the streets of the strip now looked as if they were completely abandoned. Two more shots caused Jon to duck, but they came from somewhere he couldn't see. He suddenly found himself walking up to The Bliss and who should he find there but Sheena.

"What are you doing here?" she asked him.

"Me?" asked Jon. "Didn't you hear the screaming?"

"Screaming?" Sheena looked horrified. "Of course not!"

Jon took her by the arm and quickly led her back inside the shambling casino.

"There's a problem. Someone is trying to kill me," said Jon.

Sheena wrenched her arm from his grasp and stopped him dead in their tracks. "What in the world are you talking about?"

Jon examined the casino floor for anything suspicious and leaned into Sheena's ear. "My name is Jon Burrows. I'm in danger and I need a place to hide."

She looked at him with an expression that was equal parts trepidation and attraction. "Come with me," she said.

She took him up the stairs and he was aghast to see that some of the steps had given way to rot and decay. He avoided putting his foot into the holes as they bounded to the top floor and into her room.

"The place looks nicer on the ground floor," said Jon.

"Everything does," said Sheena.

Jon agreed and she pushed him toward the closet in the corner. She opened the door and shoved him inside facing the other wall.

"You can hide in here if you have to," she said.

When Jon turned around, she was standing a little too close, and in the doorway where he couldn't move. He nearly found himself being drawn to her lips. She too seemed to accidentally lean in closer before catching herself and backing up.

"Do you think you were followed?" she asked him.

"It's hard to say. I heard other shots, but they couldn't have been meant for me. Maybe the guy got himself caught."

"How do you know it was a man?" asked Sheena.

Jon pursed his lips and thought. "Does this room have a window?"

Sheena walked to the outer wall of the room and drew back the thick curtain that looked as if it hadn't been opened in over a decade.

"Careful," said Jon. "Step back."

He placed himself on the wall to the left of the window and looked carefully down into the streets. Like a ghost town the city had emptied itself indoors. But from where he stood Jon could see the young man who had delivered him the envelope. He was bleeding out on the ground and there were members of the local police surrounding his body.

"Something must have happened. The police are at work. I think we'll be okay for a while," said Jon.

"Is that man dead?" cried Sheena as she walked forward and saw through the window.

Jon swiftly jerked the curtain closed. "You don't need to see that. Listen, can I use the bathroom?"

Sheena pointed his way, and he closed the door behind him. From his inner jacket pocket, he withdrew the envelope and tore it open. The letter was from S.O. and it detailed what his next moves were to be.

Agent Orion,

You are to leave Barley as quickly as possible. There is reason to believe that your location has been compromised. Please return to the airport and depart from the island of Tesaline. A ticket back to Arcadia will be waiting for you. Return to base.

Headmistress

Jon burned the letter with a match and left the ashes in the trash. He shook his head in frustration. "She could have told me that much on the phone," he said to himself.

"What's that?" asked Sheena from outside the bathroom door. "Is everything okay? I thought I smelled smoke."

"Everything is fine," said Jon.

He returned to her and slumped in the chair beside her table. She put her hands on his shoulders and began to massage away the knots that had been building since morning.

"You look like a man on the edge," she laughed.

"Oh, always," he said back. "I can't stay here long. I'll have to leave the island."

She walked around and faced him. "Where will you go? Who are you, Jon?"

"Who are you?" he asked in return.

She nodded and walked over to her desk. From within she pulled a gun and Jon found himself taken aback. She tried handing it to him.

"I have one," he said.

He had quickly hidden the one he carried when she met him outside of The Bliss, but now he revealed it and she marveled at him.

"Who have I gotten myself mixed up with?" she asked.

Jon smiled but jumped a little as she approached him and slowly sat in his lap. The weight of her thighs on his own sent a shiver down his spine.

"I really shouldn't have gotten you involved with all this. It could be dangerous," said Jon.

Her slender finger curled his hair as she kissed him on the cheek. "I can stand a little danger."

Jon shifted in the chair, and he locked eyes with her. It might not have been the right thing to do, but he found himself drawn to her in a powerful way. Sheena arched her back as she placed his hand against her hip.

"Kiss me," she said. He did.

When they were both finished with the pangs of passion, they sat quietly in the room for a while before speaking. Jon stood up and announced that he would have to leave.

"I guess that's all it was good for?" she asked him.

"Of course not. But I have a job to do. You wouldn't understand."

Sheena stood up and sat next to him on the bed. She placed a hand on his knee and smiled. "Try me."

"It's not that simple. I'll be flying back to Lumos, Arcadia. Once I'm there I won't be able to see you," said Jon.

She frowned but nodded. Biting her lips, she stood back up. "Then you should leave now."

Jon was startled at the suddenness of her dismissal, but he understood. He gathered his things and kissed her once more on the cheek. "Thank you for giving me a place to hide out."

"It was my pleasure," said Sheena.

"And mine."

Before walking back out onto the public floor of the casino, Jon ruffled his hair and popped the collar of his shirt. Acting casually, he moved across the room with an unusual gate that was not his own. Nobody seemed to take notice of him, and he popped outside.

The streets were picking back up. People were anxiously beginning to come back outside. Murmurs and whispers were already spreading inaccurate information and Jon caught some of it as he shuffled along. As he reached the sidewalk, he raised a hand and signaled for a taxi.

To his relief, a typically beat up yellow car pulled up beside him and he jumped inside.

"Where to stiff?" asked the driver.

"The airport, outside of the city," said Jon.

The car took off slowly and Jon kept watch on the situation outside as they passed through traffic and stop lights.

"Did you win anything?" asked the driver.

"What?" asked Jon, somewhat surprised at the sound of the driver's voice.

"Did you win anything?" repeated the man. "At the casinos, ya know?"

"Oh, no I'm afraid not," said Jon.

"Ain't that just the luck? Are you a tourist or a local?"

Jon hesitated. "Local, leaving on business," he lied.

The man seemed satisfied by his answer. "Not sure what tourists see in the place anyway. Filthy hellhole, it is."

Jon shook his head and locked eyes with the man in his rearview mirror. They both smiled.

"You ever been to the café on the corner there?" asked Jon. "Nice place."

The taxi driver laughed. "Yeah, if you like bugs in your food."

Jon kept his mouth shut. After that, so did the driver. The long journey back to the village passed in agonizing slow motion, but at long last the airport was in view. Jon paid the man and stepped out on to the curb. All seemed to be relatively quiet here.

"Excuse me? Do you have a ticket for me?" he asked the woman behind the counter at the airport service desk.

"That depends. What's your name?" she asked him.

"Jon Burrows," he said quietly.

"You're gonna have to speak up sir, I've been listening to these planes take off for years."

"Jon Burrows," said Jon, slightly louder.

"No currently booked tickets under that name. Next," said the woman.

"Hold on," said Jon. "It might be under the name…*Orion*."

The woman ran a long fingernail down a paper list of names and stopped halfway down the page. She then pulled a ticket from the drawer in front of her. "Ticket for Orion to Arcadia. Here you go."

He grabbed the ticket and moved away from her and the growing line behind him. As he boarded the plane, he kept an uneasy eye out for anyone that looked either familiar or suspicious. But everything seemed to happen smoothly.

"Anything before we take off?" asked a stewardess as Jon took his seat.

"Just a water would be nice," said Jon with a wry grin.

He pushed himself back into the chair and closed his eyes. The window seat afforded him opportunity to survey anything happening outside, but it also put him plainly into view.

"Here you go," said the woman who had taken his order.

The water was cold and crisp. As the plane began to move Jon was relieved to watch the island fade off into the distance behind him. So much had transpired in such a short amount of time that it all seemed to blur together. Still, what he would face when returning to the base of S.O. was a complete unknown. He was certain that his superiors wouldn't be happy with his performance. Especially if they knew he had accidentally involved Sheena for a brief period.

He pushed himself back into the chair and finished off the glass of water. Whatever the meeting would hold could wait until the flight was over with. For now, a decent nap would have to suffice. When he awoke, the plane had landed.

Chapter Three

"You did what?" shouted the headmistress as Jon took the seat opposite her at the desk. "How could you have involved a stranger? She could have been killed."

"Well, she wasn't. I could have been killed too, but because of her I made it back here now," said Jon.

The stainless steel that covered the entirety of the room seemed to reflect the light directly into Jon's eyes. The headmistress was glaring at him with her piercing blue eyes. The soft wrinkles around her mouth were curled into a grimace that would frighten any man.

"This is one of the most careless things you've ever done," she said. "Agent Orion, I should have you stripped of your ranking.

Jon smiled. "Well, we both know that's not going to happen."

The headmistress reeled back as if she wanted to slap Jon. "You overstep your bounds. First you pry into this mission, now this?"

"You know there's something about this one. Or you wouldn't have called me back like this. Not to mention there are people trying to kill me in the streets of Barley."

Her lips tightened so much that they nearly disappeared.

"So, what's the story? What does this all have to do with The Devil's Eye?" asked Jon.

"Maybe nothing," said the headmistress. "Maybe everything. We can't be sure."

Jon leaned back and pulled a cigar from his pocket travel-case. He lit the end and puffed on it a moment. "Typically, you're being quite vague headmistress."

"Just look at this," said the woman, passing Jon a couple of files.

Jon looked them over and flipped through the various photos and papers within. It listed two locations and a series of names that appeared to be working for the man at the top of the list.

"Who is this, *Arnoldo Trench?* I haven't heard of him before," asked Jon.

"A jewel smuggler at the top of the food chain. He was the last person we had information on relating to The Devil's Eye," responded the headmistress.

"These photographs…locations?" asked Jon.

"Yes. Pamoree and Glatana. Arnoldo was known to have set up separate operations there that both fed into each other. But we still don't know where he keeps the ruby. Or *if* he even has it."

Jon considered his options. "You must have something to go on."

She laughed. "The only other thing is that we know Arnoldo himself has been seen visiting the Pamoree plant more often than the place set up in Glatana. But we don't know why."

"It's not much. But it will do. I'll start in Pamoree."

Jon stood up and went to gather the files. The headmistress struck his hands with a quick slap.

"You can't just waltz in there like it's nothing and expect things to go right. This isn't a situation where you can shoot yourself back out," said the woman. "You'll have to be smart, Jon."

"Headmistress, I'm insulted."

He took the files and left the stainless-steel room. But he heard the door open again behind him and she leaned out to catch him.

"You will meet one of our other operatives when you land in Pamoree. He will provide you with the tools that you may find necessary. His codename is Iris. He will find you."

Jon tilted his head and winked as he walked away.

Jon wasn't happy to be visiting Pamoree. Another hot and humid land; here there were rain forests, and the sort of criminal underbelly that would make the casinos in Barley blush. But it was also home to an entirely different kind of nightlife. The sound of drums and nomadic dancers would fill the social hubs on the outskirts of the forest.

Jon took solace in the idea of his first cold drink. But when he found himself standing there and surrounded by it all, it didn't seem as sweet. The bar did not serve rum, and he was never a fan of whiskey. His entire face squinted as the burn of it traveled down his throat.

"What's the matter? Never had a real stiff drink before?" said the man serving the liquor.

"Not quite like this one," said Jon.

"Boiled it up myself," said the bartender. Jon sat his drink back down on the counter.

"That's not legal where I come from," joked Jon.

"Must be from an awful place then, mister," said the bartender, as he poured himself a drink twice as large as Jon's and swallowed it down whole.

"Yes. Sometimes it is."

Jon took his drink and turned to face the party that was happening in every direction. Men and women were dancing together. Some wearing less clothing than others, as they pressed against each other and moved to the beat. As Jon walked out of sight of the bartender, he splashed his beverage out on the ground below.

"I hope you didn't pay too much for that," said somebody from the shadows.

Jon drew his gun on instinct. "Who's there?" he asked.

The voice from the shadow revealed himself to be an older man with a thick beard. He pushed the gun back down and away. "Easy there, my name is Iris. I've been waiting for you."

Jon rolled his eyes and put the pistol away. "You could have just introduced yourself."

"I have a flare for the dramatic," said Iris.

"Clearly," said Jon bluntly.

Iris guided him through a group of beautiful dancers and to a table away from listening ears. They sat a moment, and the man revealed a bottle of rum from his jacket.

"They told me you might like this."

"Who told you?" asked Jon.

"The headmistress, of course," said Iris. "She said you get grumpy without it."

Jon smiled and took a long sip from the bottle. "I wonder how she knew the bar wouldn't have any."

"She knows everything, that woman," said Iris with a laugh. "I wouldn't doubt she can see us sitting here right now."

"I figured that's what she sent you along for. To keep an eye on me," said Jon.

They passed the bottle back and forth and Iris leaned back into his seat. He unveiled a set of car keys and threw them to Jon.

"What's this?" Jon asked.

"Plan B.," said Iris. "Should you need it."

Jon tucked the keys into his breast pocket. The rum went down like water and they both sat in the dark quiet. Finally, Iris stood up and walked them through the dirt toward an asphalt road.

"That'll be it," he said.

Ahead of Jon was the finest off-road vehicle he had ever seen. In fact, it was quite unlike anything he had ever seen before. The tires were not wide, but they were tall and grooved for traction. The chassis of the vehicle had been welded together from the ground up as a perfect roll cage.

"She'll take just about anything you can throw at her. Except bullets," said Iris.

"There's no armor at all," said Jon flatly.

"No," said Iris, pointing toward the visible roll cage and framing. "You'll have to outrun their aim. But it will get you across the terrain no matter where you travel. The fuel tanks are shielded, so you won't turn into a bomb either."

"Well, that's good then," said Jon.

Iris placed a hand on his shoulder. "This thing won't raise the alarm with the locals. They're used to creative ways to travel around here. But we couldn't send you in with a tank, could we?"

Jon shook his head. "I don't even know where you're sending me to."

"We'll take care of that in the morning. You'll be staying at a small inn. Here, I've marked it on the map." Iris passed Jon a crumpled map that had been stained with coffee. "I'll meet you there tomorrow. Then we can go over the rest of the details."

Jon climbed into the strange vehicle before him and held up the map to see in the moonlight.

"Don't do anything stupid," said Iris.

"Excuse me?" asked Jon.

"A message from the headmistress, not my words."

"Right," said Jon. "Don't be late."

Jon turned the key in the ignition and felt the power of the engine explode around him. The vehicle shook and rattled with the rumble of the motor, and Jon wrapped his hands around the wheel. With a burst of unexpected speed, he was off into the night and running. The vehicle danced around the corners and over the hills as if they weren't even there.

The wind in his face felt good. Jon even nearly forgot he was traveling to a set destination. The cruise through the night captured his imagination and he had to force himself to slow down to check the map again.

A small street lantern in the distance signaled his stop. There he found a building barely large enough to have five rooms marked *INN*. Inside, a kindly woman greeted him and gave him his room key. But before he left to locate his door, Jon heard a familiar voice speaking from the other room.

"What's that room there?" he asked the woman tending the inn.

"We have poker in there. Alcohol too."

Jon squinted his eyes as the thought occurred to him. "No, it couldn't be," he said out loud.

He moved to the door and walked through to see a room with one single poker table surrounded by three people, one of them being the card dealer. One of the poker players was a burly man who must have weighed three hundred pounds. But the other was a woman, and the sight of her took Jon's breath.

"Sheena?" he asked. She looked up with a shocked expression.

"Jon? It can't really be true, is it?" she said as she stood up to greet him.

"What are you doing in a place like this?" he asked her.

"I could say the same to you," she answered.

Jon sat down beside her at the poker table, but she motioned for them to leave. She collected whatever winnings she had earned while playing and together they headed out toward the rooms.

"I'm room four," she said.

"Five," said Jon. "I can't believe it."

"*You* can't believe it?" she asked. "I thought I'd never see you again. But here you are."

Jon opened his door and welcomed her inside. She sat down on the bed while he removed his tie and took off his shoes.

"How do you end up playing poker in a small place like this after being at The Bliss in Barley?" asked Jon, astonished.

"It's a long story. But it isn't like The Bliss is such a fine place. It's not that different from a shack like this," she said.

"I suppose. But to think we'd run into each other again. Luck is a lady after all."

She smiled gently at him and grazed his cheek with her hand. "You left so suddenly. I knew there were things I had left unsaid. I felt like when I met you something important had happened to me. Something vital."

"Yes, I too was moved by our meeting. My line of work you see…well, it gets rather hairy," said Jon.

"I saw that. Remember?" she laughed and tugged at his jacket. "Hiding you from a deranged gunman."

Jon suddenly felt sorry for her. "Did anything ever come of that? I worried for your safety when I saw the police and things on my leaving."

"I never heard another thing about any of it," said Sheena.

"That's a relief," said Jon.

With movement as majestic as a deer in the summer Sheena pushed him down onto the bed and sat over him. Her long thighs outstretched, and knees clinging to his hips.

"Do you think it can live up to our first embrace?" she said in a sultry tone.

"We can try."

In the morning she was gone. Jon hadn't even realized he had fallen asleep. He jumped to his feet and gathered his senses. When he went to knock on Sheena's door, he found it open and the cleaning lady inside. She told him that the woman who rented the room had left before sunrise.

"Are you certain?" he asked her again.

"Quite sure, sir," said the inn worker.

As he backed his way out of the room Jon bounced off the chest of Iris, who had just arrived.

"What are you doing?" asked Iris.

"Nothing. Just making conversation. I thought you would be later," said Jon.

"You told me not to be late," said Iris.

They joined each other for breakfast in the lobby of the inn. Jon had eggs, but they didn't serve sausage. Iris wolfed down several slices of toast covered in grape jelly.

"So, what's the plan? I'm growing weary of waiting for you and the headmistress to tell me what it is I'm doing here," said Jon.

"You'll be posing as a smuggler. An employee. We've got you the clothes and the alias. All you need to do is waltz in there and don't screw up your lines. Sound easy enough?" Iris asked.

"Easy?" said Jon. "It sounds like a possible suicide."

"I thought you agents were supposed to be real tough guys. Are you a coward or aren't ya?" asked Iris.

"Being tough does not mean I have to be stupid."

Iris laughed at him and took an enormous sip of his coffee. Jon smirked at how much cream Iris added to his cup.

"Look, I just help where I can. I got you everything you need to make this happen but ultimately you must do the job yourself. Your job is to get in there, look like you belong there, and then find what you need to know."

"Do you know where I should look?" asked Jon.

"Sure. Here are some photos of the trailer Arnoldo uses as his office when he visits the plant. You see that statue there?"

Iris pointed at a large bird made of concrete. Jon nodded.

"That's the key. You push that beak in, and the door opens," said Iris. "But Agent Orion, once you get inside that office; we have zero clue what you'll be facing. So be careful."

Jon eyed up the bird and the door in the photograph. He took mental note of the other surroundings leading to the trailer and pushed the picture back toward Iris.

"Thank you. Will you be here when I get back out?"

"I will be watching you as closely as I can. If anything goes badly, press this button," said Iris, and he handed a mechanical alert device to Jon.

"What's the button for?" asked Jon.

"It means we both need to get the hell out of here."

Iris stood up from the table and pushed his empty plate toward Jon. He motioned toward a non-existent wristwatch on his arm and smiled.

"I know. I'm ready," said Jon.

"Good, get dressed and get moving before I order more toast."

Chapter Four

Jon was surprised how far into the wilderness the jewel smuggling operation had set up camp. The terrain rolled up and down, and he weaved the vehicle left and right through the trees until he came upon the boulder where Iris told him to stop. They covered the vehicle with brush and leaves as best as they could before walking the rest of the way.

"Are you sure that thing will be alright there?" asked Jon. "I would have put it somewhere better.

"We need it there. Remember that boulder. We may need to find it again in a hurry."

"Of course," said Jon.

They came over a large hill and found the cliffside that lay before them was a steep climb down. It was there that Iris stopped them. He reached into the bag he had been carrying and removed a strange set of binoculars. Jon looked at them as if they were an alien instrument.

"How new to this job are you?" asked Iris.

"Newer than you, but that's obvious. How does this work?"

Iris took them back and held them to his face. His finger stretched out and tapped a button that could barely be noticed on the left side. The lens guards removed themselves from the front of the goggles and Iris handed them back to Jon.

"Fancy equipment for plain binoculars."

"What makes you think they're so ordinary?" asked Iris.

Jon held them to his face and looked out over the cliff. The goggles seemed to fixate themselves on various targets up ahead. Landmarks were zoomed in and out of focus, and each were marked with a separate color. He could see the camp of jewel thieves and each person was highlighted as they moved about. There were at least a hundred people there.

"Incredible. To think it's almost 1970 and the world has changed so much."

"You just made fun of how old I am. What do you know about the changing world?" joked Iris.

"Enough to know that this isn't street level technology," replied Jon.

Jon raised the binoculars back to his eyes and looked out toward the camp again. People were busy working. Some were sifting through dirt hoping to strike gold. Others were chipping away at rocks. On the far side away from where Iris and Jon were standing, trucks could be seen moving in with new material for the men and women to begin working on.

"This is bigger than I expected. How many of these people are common workers and how many of them are security?" asked Jon.

"Enough to know that if things fall apart you don't want to stick around," said Iris assuredly.

"I guess that's the way of it," said Jon.

Iris helped set up the spike and rope for Jon to begin his descent to the bottom of the cliff. Rock climbing was one of the more enjoyable aspects of doing the job. Jon enjoyed it.

"I guess you'll be staying up here?" he asked Iris.

"I can't climb that. Besides, I'll keep watch up here and if you need help, I'll do what I can. I have a scoped rifle up here and I'm not a bad shot. I can also get the car running if I must," said Iris.

Jon gave him a brief smile and then glanced down toward the valley floor. Taking a final deep breath, he stepped down over the side and began to slowly lower himself along the rocks. He looked back up just in time to see Iris's face vanish from looking over at him.

A bead of sweat built its way up on the edge of Jon's brow and fell softly to the dirt below. He bounced himself another few feet downward and grunted as the rope slipped around his waist. The speed of the fall increased and came to a stop suddenly, which jolted his spine and took his breath away.

"Damn," he muttered in a whisper.

As his feet touched back down on the terrain Jon sighed a breath of relief. From there he began a slow jog in the direction of the jewel camp. The trees began to spread out as he drew nearer, and he found himself bounding between each tree to use them as a buffer between himself and any possible onlookers.

"What are you doing?" asked someone Jon hadn't noticed approaching.

"Um…," stammered Jon.

"You should be working. Not taking a piss break out here in the trees," said the large man who had found Jon. Thankfully, the man was just a worker at the jewel camp, and not a part of the security force.

"I'm sorry. Where should I begin?" said Jon.

"Get up to the huts and begin chipping duty. We got a load of rocks in that the boss thinks looks promising," said the worker.

"I'll do that."

Jon continued with trepidation. He passed two members of security walking by who both carried powerful guns and were instantly distinguishable by their black matching clothes. As he snuck by, he tried to look as if he belonged there, while trying to locate something familiar from the photos Iris had shown him.

"You there! Stop walking," said a guard from behind Jon.

"Yes sir?" asked Jon.

"What's this lollygagging around? Do you think they pay you to just walk around and stare at nothing?" the guard spat.

"No sir," said Jon.

"Then get back to work already."

Jon stepped away and sprinted up a pathway that opened into a larger area full of gold hunting stations. There before him was the trailer he had been hoping to see. It was nearly forty feet away and surrounded by people, but he had found it. The bird statue that opened the door to get inside stood as if it were taunting him.

"Hello birdie," he said softly.

Trying hard to find a way to distract people away from the trailer and the statue, Jon shuffled his way into some heavy foliage and shadows. Down a path to the right, he could see a set of barrels marked with red paint. It read *TNT*.

"That's the ticket," he whispered to himself.

He removed his pistol and ran a finger along the silencer before taking aim. The barrels seemed to explode before the sound of the gun even fired. But it did the job. Workers began shouting and running away from the blast as flames erupted and smoke lifted into the sky. Guards were seen coming from all directions and going directly to the fire. Jon carefully made his way closer to the now abandoned trailer and reached for the beak of the bird.

"Open sesame," said Jon, as he pushed in the beak and the door came open. "Perfect."

He stepped inside and began sifting through drawers and boxes. But there didn't seem to be any jewels kept in here. No gold or diamonds, and certainly no Devil's Eye. He searched frantically for a safe or a lock box that he might have missed. Nothing hidden could be found.

"You fool," said a man in the doorway. "Do you think my master would keep anything valuable so *obviously* hidden?"

"Maybe," said Jon. But the man didn't find it amusing.

"You've killed yourself, whoever you are. For what purpose?"

"I came for The Devil's Eye," said Jon boldly. The man laughed in his face.

"You would never have found it here. Now my master Arnoldo is escaping away, and you are going to die," said the man.

From outside Jon heard helicopter wings beginning to turn. Things were falling apart quickly. But then it got worse.

"We've even captured your little lady friend. Quite a pretty one," said the man with a repulsive lick of his lips.

"Lady? What lady?" asked Jon, worried that he already knew the answer.

"She said that she was with you. She'll be leaving with Arnoldo now."

Jon ran into the man with such force they were both pushed through the door and back outside, just in time for him to look up and see Sheena in the helicopter as it lifted into the air. The man who had caught him squirmed until Jon was underneath and pinned to the ground.

"You've made an enormous mistake," spat the guard.

But a rifle shot echoed through the forest and the man dropped dead with a horrible thud. Jon pushed the body off himself and stood back up. People and guards were still screaming as the TNT barrels burned. But one of them took notice of Jon and began running his direction.

"Die intruder!" shouted the man as he collided into Jon.

They both shifted in the dirt, but Jon leaned into his weight and managed to stay standing as they slid backward, and the man pushed him against a tree. The man tried to elbow Jon in the face, but Jon ducked narrowly in time. He rolled through the grass and dirt and stood back up just in time to feel the man's fist collide with his jaw.

"You'll pay for this," said the guard.

"You'll pay for that," said Jon, and he managed to get in a swing of his own.

The man reeled for a second but then came back full force at Jon. They wrestled each other into a table and crashed down onto the ground. Fortunately, Jon was able to slip around the man and get him locked into a choke hold. He held tightly until the man quit moving and then returned to his feet.

"You look like you could use some air," said Jon.

His feet carried him as fast as they could back to the side of the cliff face, and he heard several more shots of the rifle fire above. More guards were noticing Jon and the rifle shots were drawing attention. He shambled to get back into the rope and started climbing his way up. One hand and foothold at a time he moved as shots fired from above and behind him.

"Come on man!" shouted Iris.

Jon pulled himself over the top of the cliff and lay flatly on the ground until Iris grabbed his hand and pulled him to his feet.

"We don't have time to lay around and nap. We gotta get out of here now."

Jon and Iris both ran back to the vehicle and began off loading the brush that had been covering it up. The engine fired and they sped away through the trees.

"What the hell happened back there?" asked Iris as he leaned around to see behind them.

"It wasn't good," said Jon.

"I can see that! You alerted the whole damn camp back there," said Iris. "Tell me you at least got the ruby."

"I'm afraid not," said Jon.

"Did you kill Arnoldo?" asked Iris.

"I'm afraid not."

Iris threw his hands up in anger and pounded the roll cage. "Then what did we come and do this thing for?"

"It's worse than that," started Jon. "I've gotten someone else involved, and her life might be in danger."

"*Her* life?" asked Iris.

"A woman I met recently must have followed me in there. I can't imagine why she would have done it. But Arnoldo himself has taken her with him and they've left via helicopter."

"I saw the bird fly the coup. Considered taking a shot at it," said Iris.

"Perhaps you should have," said Jon. "But then again, Sheena was on board."

"Sheena? That's her name? You've got to be pulling my leg," said Iris.

"I don't want to imagine what they might do to her if we can't get her away from Arnoldo," said Jon.

They pulled out from the woods and back onto a proper road. From there Jon only increased their speed. He noticed Iris gripping the side of his seat so tightly that his knuckles were turning white. But Jon pressed on with no time to lose.

"We'll see what the headmistress has to say about this. She's going to tear you a new one," said Iris.

"Maybe so, but she'll know that I have to do something," replied Jon.

As the road led them back to the small inn where they had stayed Jon put his gun away and Iris did the same. They parked behind the building and Iris got out first. Jon watched as Iris took the rifle and his bag and disposed of it in a large dumpster beside the wall.

"We have to get rid of this thing," said Jon motioning to the vehicle.

"You let me worry about that. Nobody saw what I looked like back there. You need to get out of sight," said Iris. He handed Jon a room key and pointed to the other side of the inn. "You take my room and stay in there at least until morning. Draw the curtains and don't make a noise."

"We can't waste time. I need to get to Sheena," said Jon.

"You do as I say. We're no good to her or to anyone if we're dead. Understand?"

Jon nodded in agreement.

"We're gonna do this by the book. The headmistress will tell us what to do," said Iris. "She'll call you."

Iris climbed into the vehicle and spun the tires as he peeled away into the night. Jon entered the room as directed and sat on the bed. With nothing to do, he absentmindedly began cleaning his gun. But the thought of Sheena being taken away by armed thugs crept ever to the surface. As an hour passed, he grew more restless until he thought he couldn't take it anymore.

With each passing moment it seemed that Sheena's safety would only be more in jeopardy. But suddenly the phone on the nightstand began to ring. Jon answered it.

"You're lucky I don't have Iris kill you in your sleep tonight," said the headmistress.

"You wouldn't do that. You need me to clean this mess up," said Jon, but he wasn't entirely sure.

"We're flying you out of there tomorrow and you'll be going directly to Glatana. Iris will be taking a separate means of transportation, but he will meet you there. Try not to mess up anything else Jon, *hmm?*"

Jon could barely begin to respond before she continued.

"Agent Orion? If this woman is killed because of what you've done and it becomes a public affair, you will be stripped of your credentials and put onto the blacklist of S.O.," said the headmistress.

"I…understand," said Jon forcefully.

"Good, farewell, and get some sleep."

Jon would find that last command most difficult. The night would bring nothing but tossing and turning and nightmares of Sheena at the hands of the notorious jewel baron. It would be a long restless night indeed. When he awoke, Jon was whisked away by yet another airplane leading to yet another foreign land. But the determination within himself to make it all right had never been greater.

Chapter Five

Glatana was a land of desert sands and riches amassed through the production of oil. The buildings there were all adorned with spindles of gold and were filled with people going about their religious rituals and daily routines. Men dressed in white turbans and wore as much jewelry as the women, while women often wore flowing colorful gowns that swept the floor as they walked. It was a beautiful country, and Jon liked it well.

But he wished *anything* else had been the reason for his coming here. Even sitting at a poker table felt wrong to him now. But he found himself eyeing his cards next to a few high-dollar gamblers and a stern dealer. His goal was information.

The man next to Jon was Travis Lowe, and he was rumored to have been involved in business with Arnoldo and his jewel operation several years back. But they had fallen out with a nasty argument. If Jon could manage to make friends with the man, it was possible they could come to some agreement for intel.

"You're bluffing. I'm sure of it," said Travis. His slicked back blonde hair waved as he shook his head. "I'll call it."

Jon smiled and put in even more money. Travis reared back and checked his cards again.

"I'm sure you're bluffing," he said with a smirk.

They flipped the cards and sure enough Jon had basically allowed Travis to wipe him clean off the table. The blonde man swept his winnings toward himself and laughed.

"You sir, are a terrible poker face," he said to Jon.

"You can't win all the time," replied Jon.

A beautiful woman in a purple dress that clung tightly to her ample hips approached and handed them both drinks and cigarettes. Travis thanked her and pulled out a lighter to offer a light to Jon.

"Thank you," said Jon. "To whom do I owe my thanks?"

Travis watched the woman in purple walk away a little too long and turned back to Jon. "Travis Lowe."

Jon shook his hand and tried to look surprised. "Travis Lowe. I know that name."

"Yes, well, it's been in the newspapers a bit more often than I care to admit," said Travis, as he took a long drag from his cigarette.

They both moved to step outside of the casino and onto a large balcony that overlooked the setting sun and the valley below. Jon watched as his smoke billowed out over the railing and mixed with the clouds in the sky. Travis laughed.

"I could've owned this place. All of it," he said.

"Is that so?" asked Jon. "How's that?

Travis rolled his eyes and downed his drink. He gently sat the empty glass on the guard rail and let it sit for a second before harshly shoving it over the side and watching it tumble to the streets below.

"That's a complicated story," said Travis.

"Won't they charge you for that?" asked Jon.

Travis laughed and took another puff on his cigarette. "Unlimited credit, my friend. That's the only way to play the game."

Jon nodded and considered the implications behind what Travis was saying. "You must be close to the ownership?"

Again, Travis just laughed at him. "I used to be. We were business partners. But he pushed me out."

Jon's eyes widened. "He pushed you out but pays for your gambling?"

"It's a complicated relationship," said Travis.

Jon was mentally putting the pieces together and knew that there were holes in the information he had been given that needed to be addressed by the headmistress. But he could also tell Travis was getting tipsy, and an opportunity like that was too good to miss out on.

"Would you like another drink?" asked Jon.

Travis smiled. "Trying to get me to pay for yours now?"

"I think they're complimentary," said Jon smartly.

"Oh, yes. I guess I wouldn't really know." Travis stumbled.

Jon tapped him on the shoulder and told Travis that he would track down the waitress. "Wait for me here."

Jon went back through the large glass door and windows that went into the casino and across the marble floor until he came upon a server. She was the same woman who Travis had so intently stared at as she walked away earlier.

"Excuse me?" beckoned Jon. "Can I order a drink for my friend outside?"

"Sure, what will it be?" she spoke with a sultry tone.

Jon ordered the drink and directed her to the blonde man standing on the balcony. But he himself did not immediately go back to Travis. Instead, he ducked away and located a pay phone. Quickly he shoved a few coins into the receiver and dialed the number that would patch him over to S.O.

"Hello?" said the wise voice of the headmistress. "What do you want Agent Orion?"

"It's the information on Travis Lowe that Iris gave me," said Jon. "It isn't wholly accurate."

"This better be important. It's not favored for you to call this line," said the woman on the other end.

"I know. But I was told that Travis Lowe would be a useful source to get information on Arnoldo. I was told he was a former friend with reason to help me work against Arnoldo." Jon spoke with haste.

"What are you getting at?" asked the headmistress.

"Arnoldo owns the casino where Travis spends all his time, and they give him an unlimited line of credit," said Jon.

The headmistress went silent. Jon quickly leaned out of the phone booth and scanned the balcony window for Travis. He was still standing there trying to hold a conversation with the waitress that Jon had sent. She looked uneasy.

"Headmistress, I need to hurry. What should I do next? I think Lowe is getting drunk. I could press him for information, but I don't think he will outright want to help me."

The headmistress sighed. "Get what you can out of him while he's drinking, Agent Orion. Then leave him alone and go back to Iris."

"Sounds like a plan," said Jon, and he hung up the phone.

Jon walked back out across the casino floor and hurried out onto the balcony. But he was shocked to find that Travis and the waitress were gone. His full glass sat perched atop the railing. To the left and to the right there was no sign of him. Jon glanced through the window and couldn't immediately see him in the casino either.

"Did you happen to see what happened to the man that was standing out here?" Jon asked one of the other people drinking outside.

"I'm sorry?" asked the elderly woman who was chomping on the butt of her cigar.

"The blonde fellow that was out here. Did you see where he went?" asked Jon.

"Oh, yes. I think he took that woman inside," said the lady in a croaky tone. "He had her by the arm, you know."

Jon raised an eyebrow. He rushed back through the door and followed the eyeline toward the stairs that led up to the private rooms of the casino. They were iron stairs and rose toward a sort of balcony of their own. Jon took them two at a time and quietly moved from door to door listening for any sign of Travis.

One of the rooms had the television blasting and another was stone cold silent. But the final door at the end of the row betrayed Travis. The woman waitress he had forcefully taken to his room made a sound like she was being held down and quieted. Jon kicked the door open and shut it behind him. Travis jumped off the bed, where he had been on top of the woman.

"What are you doing in here Travis?" asked Jon whimsically.

"Get the hell out of my room, pal." said Travis. "This is none of your business."

Jon and Travis circled the room while the poor waitress looked on with the blankets clutched to her chin.

"I'm afraid this *is* my business," said Jon.

Travis laughed and slammed into Jon, taking them both backward into the wall. Together the force of their impact knocked the television off the dresser stand. The glass shattered and rolled across the floor. Jon wrenched himself free of Travis's hold, but Travis drew a knife.

"Now, now, Travis," said Jon, "you shouldn't bring a knife to a gun fight."

Jon pulled his gun, but Travis moved fast. Jon felt the wind move as he narrowly avoided the stinging pierce of the blade. Travis grunted and reeled back around to face Jon.

"Who are you?" Travis asked.

Jon aimed the gun, but Travis again slammed into him and backed them both into another wall. The waitress on the bed let out a scream and Jon let go as Travis slumped down to the floor. In the haste of his defense, Jon had wrangled the knife hand of Travis backwards and forced Travis to slit himself open.

"What have you done?" yelled the woman. She jumped from the bed and returned to her dress before fleeing from the room.

"This *is* a problem," said Jon.

With little time to lose Jon searched the pockets on Travis's jacket and pants. He shoved the wallet he found into his own pocket and began listening to what was happening outside of the room. An alarm was being raised, and he could hear the footfalls of what he assumed would be security.

"I think I've just helped Arnoldo's profit margin," joked Jon to himself.

He moved for the window of the room and looked out at the rooftop that stretched out in front of him. It was the only option. He reached for the windowsill and broke the seal to let the outside air pour in. The shingling of the roof was slippery, but Jon found his footing and stepped out.

The alarm bells began ringing outside too, and Jon huddled himself close to the roof to avoid being seen. He stepped gingerly over wet tiles and dropped down to a smaller balcony than the one where he had left the drink for Travis. From there he nearly ran into a man sweeping the floor but managed to duck behind an outcropping of plants grown to decorate the casino.

Jon kept himself firmly against the shadows as he continued to move toward the city streets. Each twist and turn would bring about new risks as people moved about the casino. Guards searched frantically but didn't seem to know exactly who they were looking for. Jon played casual as he marched through the gates and out into the public.

He paused briefly behind a van while a few police officers walked by, but as he moved around the taillights a man stopped him.

"Where do you think you're going?" he asked Jon.

The man got one good shot across Jon's jaw before Jon could slide around and lock him into a tight choke. The man started to go limp, but Jon left him breathing on the road. One death was more than enough for this day. He tried not to think about telling the headmistress what had transpired.

"You!" shouted a voice as another man caught up with Jon.

"Me," said Jon sheepishly.

The man pulled out a large revolver and fired a loud shot that missed Jon completely. He fumbled with the trigger of the gun and Jon darted to knock it from his hand.

"That isn't a toy, you know?" said Jon.

They tumbled together and Jon managed to chop the man squarely in the neck, rendering him immobile long enough for Jon to run down a dark alleyway and escape.

He peeked around the corner of a building and couldn't help but to laugh at what he saw there. The nicest red sportscar that he had ever seen was sitting with the passenger side door wide open. Iris sat in the driver seat. "Looks like you've got yourself into more trouble." he told Jon.

"No kidding," said Jon, jumping into the car. "Drive."

"You're becoming a danger to me," said Iris.

"Where have you been anyway?" asked Jon.

Iris mashed the gas pedal and Jon flew back into his seat. They sped from the small road Iris had been parked on and out onto the many-laned freeway. Other cars swerved and veered out of the way as Iris steered them through the heavy traffic.

"I was waiting for you. Couldn't you tell?" said Iris, as he shifted the gears with a clunk.

"I could have used a bit of help back there," said Jon.

"Well, I didn't know you were planning on killing our informant," joked Iris.

"That's not exactly how it happened," said Jon.

The car itself seemed to grumble at Jon's lack of explanation. The engine growled and the car reached higher speeds as Iris weaved from lane to lane and finally found an exit. He slowed the car to a crawl and turned off the road into a smaller street that ran at the back of some small houses.

"Where are we?" asked Jon.

"Home base. For now," said Iris.

They pulled into a garage that was barely big enough to house the car. Iris flipped the key and the motor rattled to a halt. Jon struggled to open his door and get out without banging the wall, but Iris crashed his into the wall and climbed out without a care.

"Let's get inside quick," he said.

The inside of the house was sparsely decorated. Steel chairs surrounded a flimsy table in the kitchen and Jon checked the fridge to find it completely empty. To his horror there were no beds in the bedroom. Instead, they would be sleeping in bags that looked like they hadn't been cleaned.

"Charming," said Jon.

"I thought so too," said Iris.

He opened the closet door and tossed Jon a warm bottle of beer. He then took one for himself and wrenched the cap off with his bare hands. Jon used the side of the door jam to get his open.

"How long has this been sitting in that closet?" he asked, disgusted by the taste.

"I don't know. The headmistress sets up these places all over the world. You know how it is," said Iris.

He led Jon back into the kitchen and they sat down in the steel chairs beside the table. Jon left his beer sit there with no intention of picking it back up.

"What happened back there?" asked Iris.

"It turns out Arnoldo had been fronting our friend Travis's bill at the casino. They must have had a closer relationship than our intel thought."

Iris leaned back and sighed. "Curious."

"I found him attempting to molest a waitress. After that…well…," Jon stammered off.

"Say no more," said Iris. "Listen, this really messes everything up, and the headmistress is gonna chew your head off. But I got nothing against you stopping something like that."

Jon was surprised. "It's not like you to be okay with me going off the book."

"Yeah, well," said Iris, "I had a life before all this."

Iris reached into his shirt and pulled out a necklace with a small picture charm hanging on the end. It was of a smiling woman on a flowered background.

"Someone took her from me," said Iris. "It was ugly. He paid for it."

Jon nodded. Iris put the necklace away and headed toward the bedroom.

"Get some sleep. We'll figure this out tomorrow," he said.

Chapter Six

The smell of bacon and potatoes filled the air as Jon awoke to the new day. He rolled over in his bag and eyed the intense amount of sunlight that was pouring in through the bedroom window, then climbed up from the floor and went out into the kitchen.

"Where did you manage to get food?" he asked Iris.

The older man raised a coffee cup and smiled. "I found a place."

"I'm not a fan of bacon," said Jon.

Iris feigned being remorseful and then cracked up laughing. "Are you hungry?" he asked.

"Yes," said Jon.

"Then you'll eat," Iris concluded. "We have a lot to discuss this morning."

Jon sat down at the table and moved a large portion of the potatoes onto a plate that Iris had set aside for him. He took the bacon too, but only a couple of pieces.

"Have you spoken to the headmistress?" Jon asked.

"Yes, I have," said Iris. "She was very angry. But then we moved on and discussed strategy."

Jon smiled. It sounded like a very typical interaction with the leader of S.O.

"What did she say about our good friend Travis?" asked Jon.

"It doesn't matter. He's dead," said Iris. "Now we have half the city looking for us and they know a little bit about what you look like."

Jon swallowed a piece of bacon sideways and coughed a little. "Being a bit pessimistic now, aren't we?"

"I'm being realistic. Now, luckily, we have another person we can try to meet up with who might be more apt to help us out." Iris pulled a photo from his pants pocket.

"Alexandria Leaving. She was romantically involved with our boy Arnoldo for almost a decade. Then he dumped her and took a young bride."

"This guy is *very* charming," said Jon. "His friends are charming too."

Iris laughed. "This will be quite different."

"This woman…," began Jon. "Is she being paid off in any way? She's got reason to bare a grudge?"

Iris took an enormous bite of two stacked pieces of bacon and laughed. "Relax, kid. She's the real deal. We checked it out good this time."

"I hope so," said Jon. He took another small bite of his potatoes and sat back. "What about the young bride of his? Do we know anything about her?"

"She's dead. Dead before Arnoldo and Travis went into business together."

Jon thought for a moment. "Very interesting."

Iris stood up and chugged the last bit of his coffee. He tossed his paper plate in the trash can and sat back down to face Jon. "You gonna eat that?"

Jon pushed the remnants of his bacon across the table and took a sip of his own coffee. It was bitter and had grounds floating in the cup.

"Not the best cup of coffee, I've ever had. I'll make it next time," said Jon.

"Whatever, there's one more thing I need to talk to you about," said Iris, gravely. "This woman is strictly off limits to you."

Jon was taken aback. "Whatever do you mean?"

"You know exactly what I mean," said Iris. "These orders came from the headmistress. If you so much as bat an eye at her it could put everything at risk. No more mistakes."

Jon agreed. "She's not my type anyway."

Iris smirked. "Right."

Jon stood up and began to shine his gun with his shirt. Iris moved to the window nearest the kitchen and looked out to the streets.

"What's her name again?" asked Jon.

"Alexandria. She lives a few blocks from here in an upper-class courtyard. Money everywhere, you know how it is," said Iris.

"Sure," said Jon. "How am I to go about meeting this lovely woman?"

Iris revealed yet another interesting piece of intel. A newspaper where Alexandria Leaving had listed a job opening for a new driver. Jon could hardly believe it.

"You've got to be joking," he said. But judging by the gleam in Iris's eye, he wasn't.

"Hope you can knock that ego down a bit and play the part," said Iris, laughing.

"Very funny," said Jon.

The driveway leading up to the Leaving house was long and ornate. The gatekeeper had let Jon through along with three other contenders for the job. Jon had come dressed modestly and was keenly aware of his need to seem like a commoner. He walked less sure of himself and kept his head down, tried to seem loose, and smiled at everyone curtly.

The trees that decorated the lawn were flowered with gorgeous purple and splashes of yellow. Jon was glad he wasn't auditioning for the part of gardener.

Before being let inside, the applicants for the job were all lined up before the front door. A butler stood atop the steps and looked them all over with a scowl that caused his jowls to droop.

"You are all here to interview for the role of driving Ms. Leaving," said the butler, as if everyone didn't already know. "The good madame is accustomed to the finest and therefore you will all have to be quite impressive in order to secure the job."

"Well sir, I have a history of driving for people like Ms. Alexandria. Been doing it six years, I have," said one of the other men there. The butler grimaced.

"Ms. Leaving's former driver had been in the service for almost twenty-five years," the butler said with a shake of his head.

"What happened to him?" asked the man who had spoken out of turn.

"She fired him," said the butler.

The applicants all shifted nervously as the butler curtly turned and opened the front door of the manor. He then called the first name on his list of interviews.

"Harold Sunderland?" he called, and one of the other men went inside.

Jon stood apart from the other men. He tried to appear disconnected and aloof, but it didn't stop them from noticing him. The youngest of the pair remaining outside with Jon approached him with a purposeful lumbering stride.

"You think you're gonna get this job?" he asked.

"Maybe," replied Jon.

The young man puffed out his chest and stood as tall as possible. "I think I'm gonna get this job. What do you need it for?"

Jon looked up and quickly formed a story in his head. "I got a wife and kids at home. They like to eat."

"Yeah?" asked the young man. "Well, I need to pay for school. So, you better hope you don't get the job, or I'll find ya on the streets, huh?"

The man slammed one fist into his other hand while leaning ominously over Jon like a grizzly bear. At that exact time the butler came back outside and became aware of the young man's gruff behavior.

"You sir, we won't be needing you," said the butler.

The young man tried to protest but a few security guards from the lawn gave him a piercing look that sent the young man off the property without complaint.

"That means you'll be next," said the butler, to Jon.

After a while waiting the first man to be interviewed finally came back outside, and the butler nodded for Jon to go inside. He climbed the stairs and entered one of the finest homes he had ever seen. It was difficult to imagine a manor like that belonging to one person, and not being a hotel or a casino. Suddenly Jon felt the urge to play blackjack.

Alexandria Leaving wore an elaborate dress that looked just as expensive as the rest of her surroundings. She waved a delicate hand for Jon to join her at a wooden desk and they both sat down.

"Your name?" she asked him.

"Jesse. Jesse Aaron," said Jon. His undercover name was provided by Iris before leaving.

"Mr. Aaron. Tell me about yourself. Do you have a history of driving?" asked Alexandria.

Jon resisted the notion to laugh. "I have driven quite a great deal. But no, I have no professional history driving for folks like yourself."

Alexandria nodded. "I suppose you know that puts you at somewhat of a disadvantage compared to your competition outside?"

"I hear they have job experience, yes," said Jon.

"So, tell me why you should be my driver sir." Alexandria leaned back and lit a cigarette before placing it in a long holder and taking a brief drag.

"I assure you madame, you'll be quite safe in my charge," said Jon. He let his own voice crack through the assumed meekness of Jesse Aaron. Alexandria took notice.

"You seem like a different sort," she said. "But you aren't giving me much to go on."

Jon stood up and turned away from Alexandria. He could feel her eyes looking him over and wondering what he was up to.

"Have you ever heard of The Devil's Eye?" he asked her.

She too stood up suddenly, and Jon turned to face her. She looked furious. "Who are you? What do you want?"

"I did not mean to startle you. The truth is I know a little bit about you. I've read the papers and heard the rumors. I know your life can frequently be in danger."

She looked at him intently.

"I can protect you. I haven't worked before as a driver, but I can handle myself, and I've worked in…defensive positions." said Jon.

"You assume much," she said. "You're lucky I don't have my hired security escort you *violently* away."

"Do I look dangerous to you?" asked Jon. He moved closer and let her catch the light in his eyes. She froze.

"Yes, you do," she said.

"But do I look dangerous *toward* you?" he asked.

Alexandria seemed to be drawn closer to him, and Jon felt the attraction growing. He was breaking the rules, but it was working.

"What gives you the audacity to come in here and speak to me like this? What makes you think I won't have you tossed out?" she said.

"Like I said, I know a little bit about your history," said Jon. "I figure you might like a dangerous man from time to time."

Alexandria's eyes widened and she held a hand to her mouth. "Well, I never…"

"Never?" asked Jon. She laughed, breaking the tension at last.

"Well, maybe once or twice," she said.

Jon walked around the desk and placed his hands upon the backs of her shoulders. He felt her shiver as he moved closer and let his warm breath hit her neck.

"This is quite irregular," she said awkwardly.

"Let me help you," said Jon. "I'll tell you a secret."

Alexandria spun around and looked him square in the face. "I imagine after all this you have quite a lot of secrets I should know about."

"My name is not Jesse Aaron," he said. "It's Jon Burrows."

Her mouth dropped and she backed away slightly. But not all the way.

"I'm looking into a possible murder tied to the theft of The Devil's Eye ruby. I know you have a history with Arnoldo Trench." Jon began laying it all out on the table for her.

"You really are the most presumptive man I've ever met," she said. "What else do you know?"

"I know that you were romantically involved with Arnoldo. That he left you for a younger woman who is now dead. I assume killed, but I don't know why."

Alexandria smirked. She sat down in her chair and motioned for Jon to sit back down as well. "She was killed, yes."

"I also know that Arnoldo went into business with a man named Travis Lowe, who was killed yesterday," said Jon.

She shook her head. "I heard about that."

"What I don't understand is why Arnoldo Trench was paying for Travis to live the high life long after their business dealings concluded."

Alexandria laughed a guttural laugh that quickly died away. "And you're wondering why he doesn't pay me?"

"Quite so," said Jon.

"Does it look like I need his pity money?" she asked him. "No, I think not."

Jon cocked his head sideways. There was something she knew that she wasn't saying.

"What do you know about it?" he asked.

"Arnoldo did not like the company of women, Mr. Burrows," said Alexandria. "Travis Lowe was his lover. When their business deal collapsed, they remained closer than close, only in *private* from then on."

Jon nodded. It made sense at last.

"You've tied together a picture I couldn't quite paint myself, Ms. Leaving."

"Is that why you've infiltrated my humble job interview? To pry this trifle of information from me?" she asked.

"I'm hoping I can get more information than that," said Jon assuredly.

"Then you'll have to give something to me," she said.

"Does this mean I have the job?" asked Jon.

A short while later the two of them were standing on the front entranceway with the butler, letting the other applicants know that they were released to go home.

"You've got to be shitting me," said one.

"Tosser!" shouted the other.

Alexandria and Jon watched them leave and went back inside. She showed him up the stairs to the suite he would be calling his own. It was as finely decorated as anything else in the manor, and he even had his own telephone. Jon thanked her for the accommodations.

"Care to stay in my bed tonight? Ms. Leaving?" he joked.

"*Leaving* is exactly what I'll be doing, Mr. Burrows," she said.

With that, he was left to his own devices. As a precaution, he looked the room over for any signs of tampering or surveillance. Then he removed his tie and took a spot near the phone to call Iris.

"Hello?" said the other man on the phone. "Did you get the job?"

"But of course," said Jon. "Ms. Leaving is a lovely person with a marvelous disposition."

"You better not have gotten up to any funny business. The headmistress won't stand for anymore," said Iris.

"Funny business?" said Jon. "I'm no comedian. The important thing is I have the job and I think she'll be willing to work with us."

"Good," said Iris flatly.

"There's one more thing Iris," said Jon. "I've learned the reason that Trench was paying for Travis Lowe to live so richly at the casino."

"Oh, why's that?" asked Iris.

"They were lovers. He was never going to help us take down Arnoldo. I'm afraid our information was off."

Iris was quiet for a moment. "That *is* odd. But it's good to know. We'll have to be more careful."

"I'm always careful, Iris," said Jon.

Chapter Seven

Jon met Alexandria in her study for tea the next day. She was waiting for him wearing a rather more casual outfit than she had been wearing the day before. Even still, the room itself screamed of her wealth. Books upon books sat on shelves etched with gold that stretched to the ceilings high above.

"It's about time," said Alexandria, as Jon sat down across from her.

"I see I must wake before the sun rises if I'm to be up on your schedule," said Jon.

"I assumed a man such as yourself would do that already," jested the woman.

"A man such as I is prone to many late lights and later mornings," replied Jon.

She laughed and pushed a steaming cup of tea across the table toward Jon. He carefully gripped the fine glass and breathed in the aroma that rose from the cup. She noticed his hesitation.

"Don't tell me you prefer coffee?" she asked.

"I try not to hold preferences," Jon said, sipping the tea.

"I suppose you thought it might be poison then?"

Jon cracked a wide smile. "If you had meant to kill me you wouldn't have gone to all this trouble."

"Perhaps you're right," said Alexandria.

Her butler entered the room suddenly, and seemingly out of breath. "A letter mistress. It's about your accounts at the Federal Bank, I'm afraid."

Alexandria took the letter and read it carefully. Jon looked on wondering what was happening.

"It seems your first job is at hand, Mr. Burrows," she said, before tossing the letter into a nearby fireplace. "You must take me to the bank immediately."

"Is something the matter?" asked Jon, but she ignored him.

Together they went out into the garage and Jon felt his jaw drop at the incredibly fine automobile that was waiting for them. It must have cost nearly as much as the manor itself.

"Quite stylish," he said.

"This old thing?" asked Alexandria sarcastically.

The smell of clean leather and expensive upholstery filled Jon's nostrils as he wrapped his hands around the silver steering wheel. He started the engine and felt the smooth vibration that was almost unnoticeable. Alexandria tapped him on the shoulder from the back seat.

"Are you going to go, or do you plan to wait around here all day?" she asked him.

"Sorry," said Jon. "You'll have to tell me where this bank is. I'm not from around here."

"Oh, of course you're not," said Alexandria. "Take a right at the end of the driveway and then stay on that for a while. I'll tell you as we go."

Jon drove as steady as he ever had before as he traversed through a town that he was completely unfamiliar with. Narrow lanes and people crossing the streets without warning kept him at a slow pace. Alexandria appeared to find it funny.

"You are trying very hard, aren't you?" she asked him.

"I'm doing my job to the best of my abilities."

"Do you do *everything* to the best of your abilities?" she asked, as Jon felt her fingers grace his shoulder once again.

But the glass beside her was blown to shatters by a fired bullet that only missed her head because she had leaned forward to touch Jon. From behind them they were struck by an orange car with blacked out windows. The passenger leaned out of his window and was wearing a mask to conceal his face. Jon saw him draw a gun from the rearview mirror and quickly mashed the accelerator.

"What's happening?" screamed Alexandria.

Jon jerked the car between traffic as he tried to put distance between their car and the orange car behind.

"I'm not sure. Get on the floor if you can. Hurry!" said Jon between whips of the wheel.

Their pursuers were also skilled drivers, and Jon could see them bouncing off the other cars as they followed him from lane to lane. The gunman continued firing and innocent drivers were having their windows blown out from left to right. In a desperate move, Jon turned down a road that only had one lane.

"Where are you taking us?" shouted Alexandria through her screams.

"I don't know!" said Jon.

The orange car regretfully followed Jon's path, and together they avoided garbage cans and telephone poles as they continued the chase. Another bullet collided into the back window and cracked it severely. But it did not break.

"We can't stay on a one lane road! We're too easy of a target," said Alexandria.

"Quite right," said Jon.

He pushed the car to its limits but felt the blood drain from his face as he saw what lay ahead of them.

"I think you better hold on tightly," he told Alexandria.

The heavy expensive car hit the incline at full speed but was pulled back to the ground and in a heap. The lighter orange car however was sent into the air and sailed directly over Jon and Alexandria. Jon smiled as he watched the other car fly into the wall across the opposing street. It crumpled and the gunman in the window crashed to the ground in a nasty fall.

"Is he dead?" asked Alexandria.

"Well, he's not taking a nap," said Jon.

The car was still running, so Jon pushed forward into the other road hoping to return to safety. But Alexandria gasped. "Jon, look!"

Another orange car was careening toward them at an alarming speed. This time two gunman were leaning out of the back windows ready to fire upon Jon and Alexandria.

"Friends of yours?" he asked Alexandria.

"Are you crazy?"

Jon slammed the gas and swung around making a hard left into a busy highway. Vans and trucks swerved to avoid collision as Jon himself tried to figure out which way they should turn next. Bullets continued raining around them as the orange carload of attackers moved behind them.

"Do something!" said Alexandria.

Jon hit the brakes hard, and the car screeched to a stop as burnt rubber smoke filled the air. The orange car almost crashed into them but pulled to the right at the last second. The force of the change in direction caused one of the gunmen to fall from the vehicle. Thinking quickly Jon pulled his gun and shot the man before he could stand back up. Then Jon spun the tires as he picked up momentum again.

"Who are these men? Do you think they work for Arnoldo?" asked Alexandria.

"I think that it's very likely, Ms. Leaving."

The orange car was catching back up with them. The weight of the expensive car was holding back its ability to get away. Jon handed his gun to Alexandria, and she froze solid.

"Stay down but try to fire at them when you can," he said.

"You're supposed to be my hired protection," she said.

"I'm also your driver, and I can't do both at the same time," he replied.

Jon took a wide turn around a circle and watched behind as the orange car did the same. But Alexandria did as she was asked and fired Jon's gun through the busted window in the door. Her shots were not accurate, but they caused the driver of the orange car to make an error in judgment that sent his vehicle into a marble statue on the sidewalk.

"Very good, Ms. Leaving. Impressive indeed."

"Get us out of here," she said.

"My pleasure," said Jon.

They returned hastily to the Leaving manor and hunkered down in a centrally located room without any windows. The butler stood guard at the only door to get in. Jon thought hard on what must have happened and it all seemed rather obvious.

"The letter you received earlier. It must have been a trap. They coaxed us out of the house and then made their move. I should have seen it quicker."

Alexandria looked devastated. She too had been fooled. "It's unbelievable."

"You're absolutely sure that there have never been any signs of hostility coming from Arnoldo or his people before?" asked Jon.

"Never," said Alexandria.

Jon sighed. "Then I'm afraid it's my presence here that has caused you this suffering. They know who I am."

"How can they know?" asked the woman, as she pinned her hair back into place above her head.

"Before I came to Glatana I was involved in a bit of an altercation at Arnoldo's base in Pamoree," said Jon flatly.

"An altercation?"

"Yes," said Jon. "Well, anyway, then when I got here, I'm afraid something happened that would have put the radar out on me."

"What happened?" asked Alexandria.

"Ms. Leaving…," stammered Jon. "I killed Travis Lowe."

Alexandria seemed to be putting some of the pieces together now. "So, they must have followed you here after that."

"My thinking is that they put you under surveillance after Lowe died. A precautionary measure that proved successful. When I came here, they surely recognized me and began enacting their plan."

Jon finished speaking and sat down in a high-backed chair that felt stiff and cold. He looked up at Alexandria as she approached him.

"You seem exhausted," she said. "I was quite happy to hear about Travis getting killed, you know? Would you like to know how happy?"

She sat on his lap and twirled his tie around her finger. Jon pulled away.

"This is hardly the time," he said, barely serious.

"It's the perfect time," she whispered. Her lips were close enough to his ears that Jon could feel her breath.

"You're quite a woman, Ms. Leaving," said Jon.

"You're quite a man."

Several hours later, when Jon decided it was safe to leave, he returned to his room and made yet another reluctant phone call to S. O. He had considered calling Iris first, but the headmistress would be the one to make the final call. Jon was tired of wasting time.

"Agent Orion," said the cool voice on the other line.

"Headmistress, I have some rather interesting news to share with you," said Jon. "I also have more than a few questions."

Jon recounted the adventure of being chased by orange cars and barely getting away with Alexandria's life intact. The headmistress listened quietly and patiently until he was done. Then she spoke.

"You must extract as much information from Ms. Leaving as possible. Find out about Trench's base and anything you can about how to get in there. Then you must leave her and not return."

Jon was taken aback. "It's that simple, is it? What about her safety after I'm gone? She needs someone to protect her from this madness."

"I will send Iris to watch over her," said the headmistress. "They do not yet know his face."

Jon was miffed but satisfied. The headmistress was correct. It would probably be safer to have Iris look out for Alexandria than anything else.

"What if she doesn't want to give me any information?" asked Jon.

"You seem to have gotten closer than we wanted you to, Agent Orion. I'm sure you'll find a way to talk her into it."

"Headmistress? Are you bugging us somehow?" asked Jon.

"No. But I know *you*," the headmistress then hung up the phone.

Jon looked across his room and then went to find Alexandria.

She was waiting for him when he found her. Something about the way she held herself felt like she had reassumed a certain amount of the posh positioning she had held upon their first meeting. Alexandria was tense and stern. A small fire burned beside her, and the flashes of yellow light danced their way across her face.

"You've come to tell me you'll be leaving," she said.

"Yes," said Jon.

Alexandria folded her hands and crossed her fingers tightly. "You've brought this danger upon me only to fly away in a hurry."

"Yes," said Jon.

"Perhaps I should kill you myself," she said.

Jon did not respond. He walked around her chair and leaned over her from behind.

"A partner of mine will be taking my place. He will protect you," said Jon. "He's highly skilled and a good man."

She pulled away from his arms. "You people always think that you're in control. You're no different than Arnoldo Trench and his men."

"Excuse me?" asked Jon.

Alexandria stood to face him. Her glare shimmered in the firelight, and it made Jon step back.

"What gives you the right to do all of this? Who do you answer to?"

"We are trying to put an end to the death and greed that exists here. I did not make your decision to be with a man like Trench. Those were your choices," said Jon.

Alexandria humbled herself and stepped to face the fire. She watched the flames flicker back and forth and hung her head. "Perhaps you're right."

"I don't wish to be right," said Jon. He again moved to wrap his arms around her and this time she let him do so.

"I almost believed that this existence would go on. Never guilty and never falling. It was almost as naïve as the decision to be with Arnoldo in the first place," said Alexandria.

"We all make mistakes when we're feeling passionate," said Jon.

They faced each other again and Jon slowly pulled her lips closer to his own. They kissed just as the sound of the door opening met their ears. With a final look of understanding they pulled away from each other and turned to face Iris entering the room with the butler.

"This man claims to be with Mr. Burrows," said the butler.

"He's with me," confirmed Jon.

Iris introduced himself to Alexandria and removed the wig and sunglasses he had worn to get inside without giving away his appearance. She laughed when he did. "Can never be too careful."

"We've already been too careless as it is," said Iris, with a sideways glance at Jon.

"We need to form a plan quickly," said Jon. "Alexandria, we will need some more information from you."

"What kind of information?" she asked.

Iris began removing gadgets from his jacket and handing them to Jon. Alexandria's eyes widened.

"Jon will be going in alone. He must get to Trench and find The Devil's Eye. So, he'll need to know anything you can tell him about getting inside and where Trench keeps his closest valuables," said Iris.

"He'll never make it out alive going in there alone," said Alexandria.

"You cut me short, Ms. Leaving," said Jon. "Tell me what you know."

Reluctantly Alexandria began to describe the various entranceways and paths that she could remember. She told Jon about an elevator that went down beneath the earth where Arnoldo had set up his base of operations. If he was going to keep something incredibly valuable anywhere, it would be there.

"Perfect," said Jon. "You've been incredibly helpful."

Alexandria shook her head. "I've given you directions on how to get killed."

With a final embrace Jon exited the manor and walked out into the open streets.

Chapter Eight

Jon had perched himself atop a tree branch high above the walls of the jewel camp. He looked down upon the movements of the crowds and tried to mentally mark his position according to what he had learned from Alexandria. The sun was nearly down, and darkness would soon give him the cover he needed to begin the infiltration.

He wasn't heavily equipped. He carried his usual pistol, a few small gadgets that Iris had hastily handed him before leaving the manor, and less extra ammunition than he would have liked.

The city nightlife was beginning to bustle, and as Jon emerged back onto the public sidewalk, he could smell the wave of food and alcohol being carried through the air. Laughter and music called to him. But there was work to be done. An ornate clock at the end of the block told him it was time to make his move.

He walked the road until he came to the corner that would turn him toward the camp and paused. Slowly he backed into the foliage behind him and out of sight. The shadow of the trees above blocked out what little moonlight was still creeping out from behind the clouds. Jon knelt and made sure that his gun was fully loaded.

When he stood back up, he found himself surrounded by four large men wearing masks. They all held knives and were ready to stop him no matter which direction he tried to run.

"Good evening fellas. You get lost in these woods too?" asked Jon.

The man directly in front of him lunged forward with his blade, and Jon barely managed to duck out of the way. The man who had lunged collided into the other man who had been standing behind Jon, and they both grunted angrily.

"Lost your footing?" asked Jon.

With a feather step Jon swung around and grabbed one of the others around the throat in a solid choke hold. He could feel the man's blood pumping beneath his skin begin to slow, and his breathing became labored. With a sharp squeeze he dropped the man to the ground and faced the remaining three attackers.

"Do we have to do this? It's such a lovely night," joked Jon.

The men all moved to apprehend Jon, but he shifted and took off into the trees. Their heavy footfalls pounded behind him as he tried to evade their pursuit.

"You can't get away!" shouted one of them in a thick voice that gurgled with spit.

Jon grabbed a thin tree and swung around with his feet forward to collide into the man's abdomen. Together they crashed into the dirt and leaves. But the other two men were quick to pull Jon to his feet by either arm.

"You're dead," said one.

"I am? Thought I would have noticed." said Jon.

Suddenly Jon pulled them together and smiled as their heads banged into each other and their grip on his arms was released. By this time the third man had also stood back up and was moving in on Jon with his knife at the ready.

"You shouldn't play with knives," said Jon.

His foot barely reached but he managed to spin and kick the blade from the man's hand. In shock the man froze, so Jon took the opportunity to introduce him to a right fist. The big uppercut caught the man in the chin just right and sent him plummeting to the ground unconscious.

"You'll pay for all of this," shouted one of the remaining two men.

"Cash or check?" said Jon.

But the other two men were no longer playing around. Both tossed their knives aside and revealed guns from their holsters. Jon smiled and drew his own. The standoff lasted only a moment before one of the men stepped forward just enough for Jon to fire a shot that blasted a hole in his hand.

This enraged the remaining man so much that he charged toward Jon and tackled him into the trees and brush. The man who had been shot could be heard screaming in pain as Jon struggled to get out from underneath the one who had tackled him.

"Arnoldo Trench sends his finest regards," said the man, and he spat in Jon's face.

"I wasn't thirsty," said Jon, his eyes narrowing.

His knee busted into the man's crotch so hard that Jon could hear his soft squeal before he managed to push him off to the side. But the man with the bleeding hand was ready for revenge. Jon felt the weight of the man's elbow crash into his face and the force of it took Jon back off his feet.

"Looks like I've got a pair of fives," said Jon.

With a snap of his wrist, he fired a shot that took the fingers off the man's other hand. His screaming echoed out even louder than before as he ran off into the night. This left only one of the men still trying to take out Jon.

"You're only buying yourself more pain in the end," said the man. "You'll never win."

They came together in a grapple that saw them both shifting for mere inches as their arms quaked and shivered with the struggle. Jon finally managed to twist his hips and throw the other man to the ground. He wasted no time in jumping over him and clasping his fingers around the man's throat. When his breathing stopped Jon stood back up and took a deep breath.

"I need some air," he said to himself.

"Such a pity all I've brought you is lead," said a voice in the darkness.

"Who's there? More of Trench's pathetic men?" said Jon.

But something about this man was different right away. His suit was made of the brightest red fabric money could buy, his shoes were studded with diamonds, and his left eye was covered with a golden eye patch.

"Good Lord, what's that noise?" asked Jon. "It's so *loud*."

"Your jokes won't save you tonight, Mr. Burrows," said the man. "Yes, *we know who you are*."

Another twenty men surrounded Jon, and the man in red approached him closely. "How do you know my name?"

"The same way you know mine," said the man in a high thin voice. "Intel."

"So, you are Arnoldo Trench?" asked Jon. "What happened to the eye?"

Arnoldo brushed his thick black hair back and held a hand over his patch. He smiled. "It was truly something Mr. Burrows. You should have seen it."

Jon was increasingly aware of the other men surrounding him, but he was shiftily holding his arms to allow a tool he had hidden to fall into his hand. Arnoldo Trench seemed not to notice.

"You have killed my men, attacked my camps, and even murdered someone very close to me," said Arnoldo. "What do you have to say about such heinous crimes?"

"You should know something about heinous crimes, Trench," said Jon.

"I know that the many ways in which you will suffer are heinous crimes unlike any you've ever imagined," said Arnoldo.

Jon held up his hand and revealed the ink pen that he had clutched onto. "Can I have your autograph?"

He clicked the end of the pen, and it began emitting enormous amounts of thick white smoke. Within seconds the entire area was so cloudy that nobody could see their hand three inches from their face. Jon dropped the pen and moved through the haze being careful to avoid stumbling into the other men. But it was inevitable.

He felt his chest bump into the shoulder of one of the guards and swiftly moved to toss the man over and under. The guard yelled and Jon was sure it would draw the attention of the others, so he moved faster to get away from the source of the noise.

"You'll never get away, Mr. Burrows," shouted Arnoldo. "Even if you do, we still have your woman, *Sheena*."

Jon felt his feet stop moving as if they had plunged into quicksand. He backed himself up against a tree and began considering his options. The smoke was beginning to clear, and the only choices were to run away or to confront Arnoldo and his men.

"She truly is beautiful," said Arnoldo nastily. "It's been a real pleasure getting to know her…*physically*."

That was the final word. Jon stepped out and began firing wildly toward anyone he could see. Bullets rained upon the tree bark, but some found their target and Jon could see men slump to the ground through the remaining fog. He beelined in the direction of Arnoldo's voice, and soon the bright red fabric was easily visible amongst the white.

"You bastard," said Jon as he made contact with Trench. They both tumbled to the grass and began to wrestle.

But ultimately there were too many other men surrounding them, and a large crew of them managed to pry Jon away from Arnoldo. They held him as Trench stood back up and brushed off his red suit.

"You really think I would touch that woman?" he said. "She repulses me."

Jon realized he had been duped. The mistake seemed incredibly foolish, but he had let his emotions run away. An amateur move that Iris would no doubt criticize.

"Alright, you have me," said Jon in a defeated tone. But he had one more trick up his sleeve.

He threw a bag of what appeared to be marbles out across the dirt and they scattered amongst the men surrounding him.

"What is this?" asked Arnoldo.

But the marbles began making a horrible shriek that caused every man in the forest to grab the ears. Even Jon himself found he had to clutch his ears and try to shut the noise out. Arnoldo was writhing in pain as the noise pierced them all.

"How do we stop it?" yelled one of the guards.

"What do we do?" shouted another.

Many of them began kicking at the marbles and trying to disperse them away. But the noise afforded Jon just enough time to sneak away and begin picking off the others one at a time. One bullet here and another one there found guards collapsing to the ground while others held their ears and begged for mercy.

"Don't just stand there screaming. Kill him! Kill Burrows!" said Arnoldo as he scuttled away from the marbles and away from the gunfire.

"Coward!" shouted one of his men at the sight of him running away.

This caught Arnoldo, and he spun on his heel and put a throwing knife into the neck of the man who insulted him. He then vanished away through the trees.

Jon fired bullets between trees as he ran from position to position. But his gun was soon empty and his reloads exhausted. Breathing heavily from behind a tree for cover, he took out a knife of his own.

"Who's left out there?" he said.

There were at least seven men still standing. But they were still dealing with the pain to their eardrums and were all clearly disoriented. Jon bounded for the one closest to him and plunged the small knife directly into the side of the man's neck. He fell to the ground and Jon moved on. The next one managed to sidestep Jon before he got there, and Jon had to turn to catch his arm before a fist found Jon's face.

"What have you done to us?" said the man, as he reached for his ears again. Just enough time for Jon to get the knife into the man's hip. He fell to the ground and Jon moved on.

Two of the remaining five men ran to attack Jon together but Jon tucked to roll between them. They lost their footing and Jon swept a leg through their stance that brought them to the ground. With one graceful movement he plunged his knife into one followed by the other before they even realized they had fallen.

"Who's next?" he asked confidently.

But the largest of the three other guards managed to get ahold of Jon and put him into a tight hold. Jon felt his blood begin to pump faster before he finally was able to get free and deliver a firm knee to the man's gut. He held the knife aloft as the three men took him from left, right, and forwards.

"This doesn't have to end like this," he said to them.

The three men moved in together and Jon used the leverage of the two on his sides to lift himself up to kick the big man in the center directly in the chin. He staggered back and tripped on a stone that sent him directly into a tree headfirst. But Jon was still being held by the other two.

"What's the matter?" said the one on Jon's left. "No more fancy tools to save you?"

"Just this," said Jon. He plunged his heel into the man's foot and twisted as hard as he could.

The man on his left released his hold on Jon's arm and Jon fell into an arm drag on the other fellow to his right. He forced them into each other on the ground and got his knife into both of them. When Jon stood back up, he heard applause from behind him. Arnoldo had returned.

"Quite impressive, Mr. Burrows. Quite impressive indeed," he said.

"You abandoned your crew," said Jon. "Must be hard to find loyalty with that kind of leadership."

Arnoldo smiled a foul grin and continued walking toward Jon.

"Money finds all the loyalty I've ever needed," he said.

"I'm sure it does."

Arnold seemed unnaturally confident for a man who was no longer joined by an entire crew of security. He walked right up to Jon and looked him in the eyes.

"If you hurt me, my men at the base are instructed to kill the woman," said Arnoldo. "I know you don't want this. Either on a personal or professional front. So, surrender now."

"You know I can't let it be that simple," said Jon.

"I thought you might be bold. But you'd never get to her in time if you tried something."

"I like my odds," said Jon.

But Arnoldo finally revealed his hand, which happened to be covered with electrodes. He simply touched Jon by the nape of the neck and Jon felt his entire body go limp. He collapsed to the ground and looked on silently as Arnoldo began to laugh hysterically.

"You've been a fun little challenge Mr. Burrows, but I'm afraid this game is over, and I have won," said Arnoldo.

With another touch to the neck Jon felt his consciousness fade away and darkness took him.

Chapter Nine

Jon woke up in a room made of stainless steel. His hands were tied behind his back, and he was held up against the wall by his bindings. But the sound of movement made him jerk his head and he felt the breath taken from his lungs.

"Sheena?" he asked.

She was held captive just ten feet from Jon. He looked her over and saw no signs of bruises or violence.

"Are you okay?" he asked.

"They never touched me," she said. "But the food has been terrible."

Jon resisted the urge to laugh. "I guess I've gotten you into quite a mess."

She shook the hair out of her face and smiled at him. "Things could be worse. At least now I have someone to talk to."

Jon scanned the room for any signs of a possible exit besides the door. But there were none. He shifted to get a feel for his bindings but was disappointed to find that he had been restrained rather professionally.

"We're going to get out of here," he said.

"Oh, sure," said Sheena with a devilish laugh. "I'm glad you're so confident, but this place is like a fort."

"You have such little faith in me," said Jon. "I came here to get you out, didn't I?"

"You were captured," said Sheena flatly.

"Yes, well…," said Jon. "Don't give up on me yet."

The door to their cell opened and Arnoldo Trench walked into the room with a smile that Jon would have loved to knock clean off his face.

"Such a lovely thing to see lovers reunited. I hope you find the accommodations suitable," he said.

"What is the game here? Why are you keeping us alive?" asked Jon.

Arnoldo smacked Jon across the face. "I like to play with my food."

Sheena tried to spit on him, but she missed wildly. It made Arnoldo laugh.

"This one has been very feisty. You would be proud of her," he said to Jon.

"Cut the jokes. What are you going to do with us?" asked Jon again.

"I need to figure out who you're working for. Therefore, I will be having a team of specialists doing a number on you until you give me said information."

Jon shook his head. "You'll never get a thing out of me."

Arnoldo walked toward Sheena and grabbed her by the hair. He pulled until only one strand remained in his hand and then he yanked it from her head.

"You *will* tell me. As you can see the young woman has not been harmed during her stay with us," said Arnoldo with a grimace. "That can change if you choose not to talk."

Jon held the staring contest that had begun between him and Arnoldo. But Trench was sure of himself.

"My team will be with you shortly. Unfortunately, I have other matters to attend to. Money does not produce itself."

He left the room and Sheena screamed as she pulled on her restraints. Jon meanwhile had been working a number on his own while Arnoldo had been pontificating. To his relief they had loosened just far enough that he could get his finger and thumb between the rope and spread it wide enough to free his hand.

"How did you do that?" asked Sheena. "I've tried all this time."

"It's not my first time," joked Jon as he freed his other hand.

"I can't believe it," said Sheena.

Jon moved to get her loose. "Be quiet. We still have to get out of here before his people show up."

Jon was without his gun, and there were no tools left in his shirt to save them now. Should things turn violent he knew he would have to fight his way out, and the odds were against him then.

"Have you ever noticed anything about this room while you've been here? Are there any other ways out besides the door?"

"Are you crazy? Look around us! The whole thing is solid steel. I don't even understand how air gets in."

Jon kissed her on the lips. "Exactly," he said.

Jon licked the tip of his finger and began holding it in the air as he walked around the room. He held it low to the floor and high to the ceiling. Finally, he managed to feel a soft breeze coming from the corner of the room.

"What are you doing?" asked Sheena.

"See here?" he asked, showing her a very small crack that ran the height of the walls meeting in the corner. "There's air coming through there."

Sheena widened her eyes and began feeling the crack in the wall. "What good does that do us?"

Jon squeezed his fingers into the crack as hard and as far as he could. Then he began to pull. "Help me there," he said.

Together they pulled and Jon began to feel the thin sheet metal begin to give. He urged her to keep going and before they knew it the walls had peeled away to reveal boards and plaster. But there was also an air shaft.

"Thank God," said Sheena.

But voices could be heard approaching and Jon shushed her. He waved for her to get to other side of the room and Jon positioned himself just beside the door. When the two guards entered the room, he surprised them and slammed the door shut behind them. They tried to resist but Jon was faster and quickly began punching them both until they lay bloody on the floor.

"Are they dead?" asked Sheena.

"Of course not. But they're missing a few teeth now. Might be an improvement on those mugs," said Jon.

He ushered her toward the air shaft and told her to go first but she refused.

"Are you insane? We have no idea where this goes or who might be waiting on the other side!"

"You might be right," conceded Jon. "I'll go first. But stay close."

The venting was just big enough for them to crawl through. Jon winced with every forward motion that rang out against the metal and seemed to echo through the shaft like a cavern. Sheena followed behind him carefully.

"There's a fork up ahead. Do you fancy we go left or go right?" asked Jon.

"Why are you leaving it up to me?" replied Sheena.

"I thought it polite," said Jon. "We'll go left."

The ventilation stretched out in front of them for quite a way, and they crawled until Jon felt his knees getting sore. Finally, they came to a grate that dumped out air below them.

"It's a bit of a drop to the floor. I'll go first and then I can catch you when you come down," said Jon.

"How do you know what we're falling into?" asked Sheena.

"I don't. But the room below looks dark, and I can't hear anything. We might have gotten lucky."

"I don't like playing on luck," said Sheena sternly.

"Neither do I. You know I threw that card game with you when we first met. I wasn't playing on luck," said Jon.

He removed the grate and dropped through the hole to the ground below. The room was dark, but he thought he could make out a bunch of old desks and paperwork scattered about. He looked back up and waved for Sheena to follow him. She dropped into his arms, and he placed her safely on her feet.

"Where do you think we are?" she asked.

"Some kind of office space. It doesn't look like they use it anymore."

"I wonder how far underground we are," said Sheena.

Jon suddenly realized she was onto something. He had been unconscious when they brought him to the cell, but Sheena had been awake.

"Are we underground? Are you certain?" he asked her.

"Quite sure. They took me to a large elevator that seemed to go down for ages. Then they ushered me through one of the largest empty rooms I've ever seen and down a long hallway to the cell we were in."

Jon nodded. "So, if we've just dropped down from the air vent, we're another floor down."

"That sounds right to me. Why?" asked Sheena.

Jon moved through the strange office and stopped at the door. He cupped his hand and tried to listen for any noises on the other side. Sheena pushed against him and attempted to listen as well.

"I was told that this base had an elevator that led down to Arnoldo's personal suite. It might take us to where he keeps The Devil's Eye," said Jon.

"The Devil's Eye?" said Sheena in shock. "Shouldn't we just focus on getting out of here with our lives?"

"It's more complicated than that. My entire mission hinges on me finding The Devil's Eye, and tracing the murder I've been following up on to Trench and his gang."

Sheena backed away from him and shook her head. "I see."

Jon opened the door and saw that it led out to a darkened hallway littered with trash. He went out first and took another left toward another door with a frosted window. Jon tried to see through the glass but to no avail. Sheena joined him beside the door.

"We could be a hundred hallways away from where you're wanting to be," she said. "We have no clue where to go."

Jon pursed his lips. "Not exactly true. I have some information to go on, I just have to find something that looks familiar."

"A sign post?" jested Sheena.

Jon opened the door with the frosted glass just a crack and was surprised to see light on the other side. A much grander hallway lay opposite the door; obviously decorated with Arnoldo's expensive taste in mind. Golden trim and lavish paintings adorned the walls. Jon quietly cracked the door and turned to Sheena.

"This is it," he said.

"Is what?" she asked.

"The main hallway from the elevator to Arnoldo's saferoom," said Jon.

Sheena grabbed her head with both hands. "There must be guards out there!"

Jon squinted his eyes and wobbled his head. "I don't hear any," he said. "I don't see any either."

"But there must be!" said Sheena.

Jon agreed. He instructed her to remain behind in the dusty hall while he moved through the door and into the other side. He nearly held his breath to keep from making noise, and his every move was slow and deliberate. The door had let him out just next to the elevator and the fancy hallway stretched out until coming to a door that was covered in mirror glass. Jon fixed his tie and turned the handle.

It swung open slowly and Jon could neither see nor hear anything on the other side to be alarmed over. He turned back toward the only other door in the hall and called for Sheena.

"Is it safe?" she asked in a loud whisper.

"Safe enough," said Jon. "Hurry up."

The room inside was not nearly as big as Jon had imagined. But it was outfitted in some of the finest decoration that he had ever seen. The oak desk that sat across from the door looked hundreds of years old and just as sturdy as ever. The chair was made of the finest leather, and the artwork on the walls were famous paintings Jon thought he recognized as being famously missing or stolen.

"Incredible, really," said Sheena.

"Maybe," said Jon. "But remember how he got all of this and it's not so impressive."

"What are we looking for?" she asked him.

"Check the drawers on the desk. I'll look for a safe," said Jon.

Sheena rummaged around in the desk for a while and Jon checked the file cabinets for any lock boxes or personal safes. But both came up empty.

"Check behind the paintings," said Sheena.

"Good idea," said Jon, and sure enough he located the large safe built into the wall hidden behind the first painting he pulled down. "Clever girl."

"Sometimes I surprise myself," said Sheena.

"But we'll need to find a way to open it," said Jon.

Sheena nodded and began going through the desk again looking at paperwork for any signs that Arnoldo may have jotted the combination down somewhere. Jon pondered if there was any way to pry it open.

"If I still had my gun and tools this wouldn't be an issue," he said.

Sheena ignored him and continued dumping papers out of drawers onto the top of the desk. Then she let out a gasp.

"Jon, look!" she said, with a finger outstretched toward the bottom of the drawer she had been going through.

"You really are something else," said Jon. He leaned in and kissed her softly.

The numbers to get into the safe had been stamped into the wood, and Jon speedily dialed them in and cracked it open. Inside were more stacks of money than Jon could have imagined, and they were all surrounded by various loose jewels. Diamonds, sapphires, even amethysts. But no rubies, and certainly no Devil's Eye.

"Blast it," said Jon. "Where else would he keep something like that?"

Just then an opening on the ceiling was revealed and a small slender television monitor slid down into their view. It flipped itself on and they found themselves looking at Arnoldo Trench on the screen.

"You lovely fools have truly doomed yourselves now," he said. "Were you really so daft to think I would keep The Devil's Eye in such an obvious hiding place?"

"Can he hear us?" asked Sheena.

"Of course, I can hear you!" said the image of Arnoldo on the television. "In just a few moments the alarms will sound all across my facility, and every guard I have on hire will be heading your direction."

"You won't get away with this Arnoldo. We know you keep it here somewhere," said Jon.

"Would you like to know where?" asked Arnoldo with a snicker.

Jon and Sheena watched in horror as the man on screen removed the eyepatch from his face. Underneath he revealed that The Devil's Eye had been implanted in his own socket. The shimmer of the ruby in the light glared through the camera lens and seemed to stare at Jon taunting him.

"Ingenious," conceded Jon. "I should have guessed it."

"It is ironic, isn't it?" said Arnoldo. "The Eye goes with me, Mr. Burrows."

The room was suddenly filled with the sounds of alarms going off outside and on the television. Lights began to flicker and flash, and Sheena pushed into Jon's arms.

"Have a nice death, Mr. Burrows," said Arnoldo. "I'll be watching."

He began laughing and Sheena pounded her fist into Jon's chest. "What are we going to do?" she asked.

"We'll figure out something," said Jon.

The television turned itself off and retracted back into the ceiling. Jon held Sheena only for a moment and then tried to get her back into her senses.

"We can't stay here," he said. "We must try and find my weapons. Or *any* weapon."

"We're both going to die," she said.

"Then we'll die fighting," said Jon.

Chapter Ten

By the time they exited the room back into the elaborate hallway, men were already pouring out of the elevator. Jon practically forced Sheena back into the trashy hallway and tried to block the door behind them. He then urged her to go back into the dusty office room and helped her climb back up into the air ventilation.

The sound of beating fists and shoulders could be heard on the blocked door outside as Jon himself propped himself up on a desk and climbed back into the shaft.

"Now what do we do?" asked Sheena.

"Go back the other way. Where we took a left, keep going the opposite direction."

She began crawling and Jon followed her as the sounds of approaching voices grew louder. They would have surely entered the office room by now.

"There, what's that up ahead?" he asked Sheena.

"It looks like another corner vent like the one in our cell," she answered.

"Kick it," said Jon. "Kick the hell out of it."

Sheena began beating on the sheet of metal until it started to move. Jon squeezed himself in beside her and began kicking it as well, and before long they had gotten out into another room.

"Where are we now?" asked Sheena, as the sounds of men crawling in the vents continued to approach.

The room was filled with tables covered in brush kits. It was tools for cleaning jewels and evaluating their value. "It's the processing area," said Jon.

Sheena's eyes glistened and she began rummaging on a table looking at all the shiny jewels that lay scattered about. "There's so many."

"We have to get to the room where they're keeping my gun," said Jon. "There must be a storage room somewhere."

Jon walked out of the processing room and into a square room with four doors. One for every wall. The one to his left was marked *Bookkeeping*. The one directly facing him was marked *To Elevator*. But the one to his right was clearly marked *Storage*.

"Fingers crossed," said Jon, and he grabbed Sheena by the arm and entered the room.

At least a hundred lockers lined both walls left and right. But in the center of the room was a large ancient chest being held closed by an equally old lock. Jon took his foot and bashed on the lock at just the right spot and felt his heart leap as it tumbled to the ground. Inside the chest he found his .22 HDM and the only other gadget that Iris had managed to give him.

"We're going to make it out of here Sheena. I promise," said Jon.

"I'm still not convinced," she said.

Jon held a finger to his mouth and asked her to be quiet as the voices from outside the room swelled to a fever pitch.

"Which way did they go?" asked a rough voice from just outside the door.

"Maybe to the elevator?" asked a high voiced man.

"No, he'll be trying to get his weapon back. No doubt," said a third voice.

Jon waited and motioned for Sheena to get down. As he watched the doorknob turn, he gripped the gun tightly between his fingers. Without any ammo left he sprang into action as soon as the door swung open and clunked the first man square in the forehead with the butt of the gun.

"Stay down!" he yelled at Sheena as she moved to get farther away.

The man with the high voice yelled and cracked both his hands into Jon's back so hard that it staggered him. But Jon ducked before he could get another shot in and was just able to sweep the man's legs.

Jon then knelt over him and began beating him with the gun until he had nothing left.

"Jon, lookout!" shouted Sheena.

The third man was nearly ready to take Jon out with a football style tackle, but Jon leapt over him with precision timing. His hefty frame crashed into the lockers on the wall and left a large dent in several of them.

"Don't let him up!" said Sheena from afar.

Jon again used the end of his pistol to bash the man in the cranium until he fell motionless to the ground. Jon then searched them all for ammunition and managed to scrape up nine bullets.

"Come on," he said to Sheena, and they headed for the elevator door.

They arrived just in time to greet two other men as they exited the lift. Both carried AR-18s, and Jon had to be fast on the draw to get them dealt with before they could begin blasting the hallway with bullets. As they fell to the ground, he felt Sheena squeeze his other hand.

"I thought they had us," she said.

Jon picked up one of their guns and handed the other one to Sheena. She looked at it as if it were an alien object. "Just in case," said Jon.

"If you say so."

They walked into the elevator and pressed the button leading up to the ground floor. Jon positioned himself just on the edge of the door and instructed Sheena to do the same. The ride up was slow and shaky, and he could hear nothing but the sounds of their nervous breathing.

"Now!" shouted Jon as the door opened, and both he and Sheena stepped out and began shooting their newfound weaponry.

They weren't taking the time to aim at anything, but the spraying bullets provided them enough cover to get out and find shelter behind a large truck. They found themselves in the middle of a large lot of vehicles and barrels filled with gasoline or oil.

"We must be careful. Don't get too close to the barrels," said Jon.

"Do they explode?" asked Sheena.

"Well, they're not filled with water."

Jon leaned out and shot a man who was standing above them on a guard rail. He fell to the ground below but from somewhere else another shot nearly found Jon. Luckily, he ducked back behind the truck and avoided his death.

"What are you waiting for? Fire that gun. Give me some cover!" he said.

Sheena just barely held her gun around the corner of the truck and began shooting blindly. Jon stepped out from his position and managed to fire two shots that found their targets. But more men were all around them.

"We need to get away from here," he said.

"Where do we go?" asked Sheena.

Jon looked around the base and took notice of the helicopter far away in the distance. "There! We have to fly out of here."

"It's so far," said Sheena.

"Would you rather be killed?" asked Jon, as bullets ricocheted on either side of them. "We have to go."

In between the sounds of incoming rounds Jon and Sheena ran together across the asphalt. Jon shot off only a few shots as their focus became movement. But as they vaulted over a rail and onto another platform, they were met by five other people. They were being led by a woman who was well over six feet tall.

"You will not escape this camp," she said. "You are completely surrounded."

Jon held his hands up and Sheena did the same.

"Does your boss know what we have stolen from him?" asked Jon. Sheena looked at him confused.

"What are you talking about?" asked the tall woman commander.

"I have a box full of his most valuable jewels. It's here in my pocket," said Jon.

The woman was apprehensive but obligated to investigate. She walked forward and began searching Jon until she found the medium sized box that had been hidden in the chest with Jon's gun. She investigated it carefully and returned to the line of other gunmen.

"How do you open it?" she shouted.

"It's the button on the side," said Jon.

As the tall woman fumbled with the box Jon waited until the optimal moment. He then pushed into Sheena and they both hit the ground as the tall woman found the button and the box exploded in glorious fashion. Her and her unit were both swallowed up in the flames as Jon and Sheena rolled away.

"You could have gotten us killed!" said Sheena.

"We were about to be killed regardless," said Jon.

Jon helped her back to his feet and together they continued across the compound. A man in sunglasses stepped out around a corner to stop them but Jon was quicker and managed to throw him to the ground in a matter of seconds.

"We have to keep moving," said Jon.

Just then a public address system began to speak. It was Arnoldo's voice. "You are making a grave mistake Mr. Burrows. You will get yourself and the woman killed."

Nearly ten men suddenly came running up and surrounding the perimeter where Jon and Sheena were waiting. But keeping his wits about him Jon led Sheena to one of the nearby trucks and they climbed into the cab. Jon bashed the dash open with his fist and began wiring cables together.

"Hurry up down there!" shouted Sheena.

The truck roared to life and Jon mashed the pedal to the floor. He jumped up and grabbed the wheel as the truck plowed through gating and fences. Men were yelling and shooting from either side, but Jon refused to slow down. A couple of guards barely leapt out of the path of the big rig.

"You missed them!" said Sheena.

"They got lucky," said Jon.

He kept a steady line toward the helicopter pad on the far side of the camp, but they still had a long way to go, and the truck was slow. Sheena ducked down into the floorboard as a bullet pinged her passenger side door.

The old truck was tough, but it had its weak spots. The guards were well aware of this and began focusing their fire on the front of the truck. Jon knew that soon enough the radiator would be filled with leaking holes and possibly gas lines would be shot to bits. He pushed the truck as hard as he could until he felt it begin to wind down and came to a rolling halt.

"Why are we stopping?" asked Sheena.

"Get out on your side. We'll use it for cover like before," said Jon.

They both stepped out and Jon instructed Sheena to provide cover fire as he stepped out and took out a couple of guards. But the pressure was mounting as more and more men began appearing out of the woodwork.

"There's just too many of them! You can't kill them all," said Sheena.

As she said it her gun ran out of ammo. Jon looked over his shoulder and sighed. He took out his pistol and handed it to her. "Don't shoot unless you have to."

She held the pistol slightly more confidently than she had originally looked at the bigger gun. Jon checked his own ammo stock and then checked to see how far they had to get to the helicopter pad.

"Jon!" said Sheena suddenly. "The barrels."

Jon looked out and saw what she meant. From their new position they were away from the barrels of gasoline. But the men shooting at them were dangerously close to the readymade explosions.

"You're the best," he said. With a few quickfire shots he watched as the plumes of fire rose into the air and bullets quit flying. The smell of smoke began to sift through the camp and Sheena laughed.

"It worked! I can't believe it actually worked." she said.

"We don't have any time to waste. There will be more of them," said Jon.

Sure enough, a man with a knife came around the corner of the truck and attacked Jon directly. His fist landed in Jon's ribs like a bomb hitting the dirt. Jon felt the breath pulled from his body and he gasped for air. Sheena began to take aim, but Jon forced out a "Don't shoot."

"I can do it," she said. But it drew the man's attention to her.

Jon lunged and muscled the man away from Sheena. They bounced off the truck and rolled from one position of power to another until Jon could get him to the ground. His pounding punches busted his knuckles open, but the man quit moving.

"Run," said Jon to Sheena.

Together they ran as the terrain changed from asphalt to concrete and then finally to grass. But just before they could reach the stairs that went up to the helicopter pad they were pinned down by another group of Arnoldo's soldiers. They hunkered down behind a stone wall that gave them cover from both directions, but Jon was nearly out of bullets.

"You're gonna have to help," he said.

Sheena cocked back the hammer of the gun and together they knelt up to shoot. Jon picked off a man across the way and to his surprise Sheena made a perfect shot at another man on the other side.

"You're quite a shot with that thing," said Jon.

"Sometimes I surprise myself," said Sheena, as she had earlier.

Jon took out man after man. But the incoming bullet barrage kept coming. Sheena fired a few more rounds, some successfully bringing a man down, and others missing wildly.

"I'll take that fellow on your side and then you make a run for the helicopter. Got it?" said Jon.

Sheena nodded affirmatively and Jon took the shot. Sheena darted toward the stairs, and he watched as she disappeared above him. Jon's gun was nearly empty, and he used what little ammo he had left to provide himself cover fire as he too ran up the stairs.

"How are you going to start this thing?" asked Sheena as Jon tried to open the door to the cockpit. It didn't open.

"Damn it!" he said. "Give me a brick or a rock or something."

Sheena searched around the pad and found a piece of concrete that had broken off the building. The few guards that were left were closing in on them and Jon quickly busted the handle off the helicopter door. It swung open and he climbed inside. But the small group of soldiers were at the top of the stairs.

"Get this thing moving!" shouted Sheena.

"I'm trying," said Jon.

Sheena took aim and brought the men down. They slumped to the ground right as the blades on the helicopter began to spin. She held her head down and climbed in through the door.

"I think we got them all," she said.

"Not all of them, I'm afraid," said Jon flatly.

"What do you mean?" she asked.

Jon held his finger aloft, and just at the front of the helicopter stood Arnoldo Trench in his bright red suit. His gun was directly aimed at Agent Orion's forehead.

Chapter Eleven

"I have battled other crews. I have fought the law. But never has anyone or anything caused me so much trouble as you, Mr. Burrows," said Arnoldo.

"It was my pleasure," said Jon. "I like to think I'm not finished just yet."

Arnoldo cackled. "You are finished. Dead to rights. Step out of the helicopter or be killed."

The sound of the spinning blades was nearly deafening. Sheena seemed ready to exit the helicopter and surrender, but Jon had not given up just yet. He pushed the chopper forward and nearly trampled over Arnoldo Trench. But the man in the red suit was strong, and he clutched to the feet of the helicopter as they began to rise into the air.

"What do you think you're doing?" asked Jon. "You didn't show me your ticket!"

Arnoldo began shooting and Jon sat back too quickly. His whip of the controls sent the helicopter dipping to the left and Arnoldo slipped to hanging on by one hand.

"You'll get us all killed!" he shouted up at Jon.

"Just let go then!" Jon got ahold of himself and leveled out the plane of their flight. Arnoldo managed to climb himself back onto the footrail of the copter and was hanging on for dear life.

"How are we going to get rid of him?" asked Sheena.

"I'll think of something," said Jon.

He pushed higher into the sky but watched in disappointment as Arnoldo began to work himself toward the door. Jon tried to wave to the left and dart to the right, but Arnoldo was getting closer and closer to getting inside.

"He's gonna get in here!" screamed Sheena.

Jon got the helicopter into a hovering position and sat Sheena down at the controls. "Keep it steady. Nothing else."

She gulped, and he went back toward the door just in time for Arnoldo to knock him in the head with a right hook. The chopper rocked gently as Jon stumbled and Arnoldo aimed his gun.

"Why won't you give it up?" he snarled.

Jon brought his right foot into Arnoldo's gun and watched it fly out of the helicopter to the ground below. The vein in Arnoldo's face began to pump so hard it was easily visible. With a roar he dove into Jon, and they started grappling. The helicopter began to move in the air in each direction they tumbled, and Sheena was struggling to find the proper adjustments.

"Maybe we'll all go down together, Mr. Burrows," snapped Arnoldo. "Wouldn't that be something?"

Sheena had thrown the helicopter into a soft descent and the ground was approaching. But they were also moving forward at a decent rate of speed. The crash was not horrific, but it was a hard jolt. The glass shattered and metal was bent. The blades dug themselves into the muddy ground they landed in. Jon banged his head pretty good as he was thrown from the wreck, and Sheena sustained a gash to her shoulder.

Arnoldo was bleeding from the mouth but was the first back to his feet. He grunted and groaned as he backed his way up against a tree to hold himself up.

"What have you done to me?" he asked. "I had power here! I will kill you with my bare hands."

Jon pushed himself up and stood between Arnoldo and Sheena. He held up his fists and the two men circled each other amongst the bent steel and broken glass. Sheena took the opportunity to crawl out of sight and away from the fight.

"You dealt in death and suffering for years Trench. The power and wealth you built was never going to last forever," said Jon.

"I will still rebuild," said Arnoldo.

"Your greatest mistake was going after The Devil's Eye. After you killed that man, I heard him say the word *ruby*," said Jon.

"What man are you talking about?" asked Arnoldo.

"The man in Tesaline. I was there that night," said Jon. But Arnoldo seemed confused.

"I never killed a man in Tesaline. I have had this precious ruby for a long time," said Arnoldo. "You've been on a goose chase."

Jon shook his head. "Whatever you say."

They clashed and Jon reached his left arm around Trench's head. He squeezed down, but Arnoldo had better footing and pushed Jon into a tree. Two powerful punches struck Arnoldo in the jaw, but he still managed to wrestle free from Jon's hold.

"You're fast," said Arnoldo. "But foolish."

He backhanded Jon and the ring on his finger left Jon's cheek stinging in pain. Jon grinded his teeth and delivered a two-count combination of jabs to Arnoldo's ribs.

"What's the matter Arnoldo? Can't breathe?" asked Jon. "Those were your ribs I felt cracking."

Arnoldo clasped his non-dominant hand to his ribs and backed away from Jon. He snorted and spit. "You're ruining my suit."

Jon made a run for it and swiftly took Arnoldo off his feet. With a fluid movement Jon rolled to grab his arm and clench it down.

"I can break it. You know I can," said Jon.

"Do it then," said Arnoldo, and Jon obliged.

The sound of it snapping even made Jon feel a bit sick to his stomach. Arnoldo screamed through gritted teeth and looked up to the sky. He ripped the eye patch from his face and let the light catch the ruby in his head.

"You'll *never* take it from me," he said.

Suddenly he twisted and drove his good fist into Jon's crotch. It sent Jon doubling over and gave Arnoldo enough time to stand back up. He stood over Jon and began kicking him in the face and stomach. Jon felt his muscles tighten and beg for mercy with every impact but couldn't get away from the kicks. He rolled away but found himself propped up against a tree stump. Arnoldo had the advantage.

"What's going on here?" said a voice that Jon couldn't have been happier to hear. It was Iris.

"Iris? What are you doing here?" asked Jon, from the ground where he was laying.

"This loon had the manor bugged while you were driving Alexandria. They knew I was sent in to replace you," said Iris. He stepped forward and Alexandria was with him. "We had a bit of an altercation and then came here. We saw the helicopter fall out of the sky and thought you might need some help."

"You people will die!" shouted Arnoldo. He tried to attack Iris but stopped at the sight of a gun staring him down.

"How do we get the ruby out of your face, bud?" asked Iris.

"No. You can't take it from me!" said Arnoldo, clawing at his own face.

Iris motioned for Alexandria to stand back and pressed the barrel of his weapon into Arnoldo's cheek. "I'll only ask you one more time. How do we get it out of your face?"

Jon stood back up and came up behind Arnoldo, leaving him no way to run. Iris twisted the gun, but Arnoldo showed no signs of weakness.

"You won't take it from me," he said.

Suddenly Sheena reappeared over the top of a small mound and aimed Jon's pistol directly at Arnoldo. "What are you waiting for? *This* is how you get the ruby back."

She shot Arnoldo through the skull.

Jon and Iris both spun on their heels and looked around in horror at what happened. Confused and disoriented they looked at each other for answers as Sheena marched between them and knelt over Arnoldo's dead body.

"Now all I have to do is take it," she said, and she began to pry The Devil's Eye from Arnoldo's head.

"Jon? What the hell is happening here?" said Iris. He pointed his gun at Sheena and then at Jon.

"I don't know!" said Jon, pushing the gun away.

Iris turned to point it back at Sheena, but it was too late. She had stood back up with the ruby in one hand and Jon's gun in the other. She waved it in Iris's face and told him to drop his gun.

"Sheena? What's going on?" asked Jon. "What are you doing?"

She bounced the ruby in her palm and smiled devilishly. "You helped me get this. I should be thanking you."

Jon couldn't understand what she meant.

"After I killed that man in Tesaline I barely had any information at all. But I tailed you after you left that night," said Sheena. "After that it was simple."

"What are you saying?" asked Jon in horror.

"My name is not Sheena. I am *Ruby Windego,* and I have been searching for this priceless gem my entire life. You brought me to it."

She smiled and tucked the ruby away. Never wavering on keeping the gun pointed at Iris she backed away from the group and laughed.

"I'm almost sorry about it. We had some fun," she said. "Goodbye Jon."

Jon went to move but Ruby fired a shot in the direction of Alexandria Leaving. The bullet caught her in the shin, and she fell to the earth.

"Ms. Leaving!" shouted Jon, and Ruby vanished away from them.

Jon rushed to Alexandria's side but Irish pushed him away. "I've got her. Go after the woman; you can catch her if you hurry."

Jon ran from the wreck of the helicopter and into the woods. He saw no clear signs of where Ruby had gone but he figured she couldn't have gotten too far away.

"Sheena!" he yelled. "Or Ruby. Whatever your name is…"

He thought he heard something move behind a large bush and he spun around. But it was nothing.

"You won't get away with it," said Jon. "If not me then someone else will come for you. Maybe I can help you get off easy."

This coaxed a laugh from the distance and Jon moved in its direction. He checked behind trees and over boulders but saw no trace of the woman.

"Is this how you treat me after letting you win that game of poker? I thought we had something special," said Jon.

Out of nowhere a couple of Arnoldo's remaining men appeared, and began to head toward Jon. He shifted his weight down to one knee at the last second and gave one a toss over his hip. The other he tripped.

"I thought I was finished with you guys," said Jon.

"Where is the boss?" asked the man Jon had tripped.

"I'm sorry to tell you he didn't make it," said Jon.

The two men became enraged and grabbed Jon by the shirt collar. "You killed the boss?" asked one of them.

"No. But I wish I did!" Jon began kicking until he could get pulled away from them. He found a limb that had fallen from a tree and used it like a baseball bat. The end of the wood smacked one of the men in the face so hard that Jon could see his teeth go flying.

The other man moved for Jon but again was blasted by the end of the limb. "The woman who killed your boss is in these woods," said Jon.

"Yeah, right," said the man with the missing teeth. "You expect us to believe that?"

They both grabbed at Jon, but he spun with the tree limb in his hands and cracked them both in the skull from opposite directions. One of them fell to the ground but the other stayed standing.

"You could help me stop her," said Jon. "Or you can end up like your friend and everyone else at this jewel camp."

The man thought about it for a fraction of a moment but decided against the better judgement. He plunged at Jon like a tank. Jon broke the stick across the man's face and followed it up with an uppercut that stole away his consciousness.

"They should hire better help around here," said Jon.

As he continued running, he came upon an incline that went back down toward the camp. He peered across the hillside and thought he could see the shape of Ruby running for the gates. There were several vehicles down there waiting for her to make an escape with if Jon couldn't catch her in time.

"Dammit," he said, before breaking into a hard run.

There were still a few guards left at the facility, and they tried to stop Ruby. But as Jon came down the hill toward the gate, he was amazed to see her holding her own in a physical confrontation. She kneed a man in the stomach and bashed him with the bottom of Jon's gun.

"Ruby!" shouted Jon. "Stop running!"

She knelt over the man she had wounded and searched his pockets. When she stood back up Jon froze in his tracks as she waved a set of keys in his face. She kept the gun aimed at him.

"I liked you. Really, I did," she said. "But if you keep following me, I promise that I will kill you."

"You know I can't let you get away," said Jon.

She smiled a crooked smile and backed her way into the car behind her. She turned the key in the ignition and kept the pistol on Jon until she could pull away. When she was far away and fast enough to be safe Jon bolted for the other car and began to hotwire it. As soon as it started, he nailed the throttle.

Jon watched as Ruby bounced her vehicle off a guard rail and began to peel down a road leading into the trees. He followed her until he saw Iris and Alexandra making their way along the side of the road. He grinded the car to a stop and let them both inside. Alexandria was barely able to walk, but Iris had done a fair job at bandaging the hole in her leg.

"Is she going to make it?" asked Jon.

"She'll live. But we better stop that woman with The Devil's Eye, or the headmistress will have our heads," said Iris.

By this time, Ruby was well ahead of them, but Jon pushed the car to its limits. He could hear Alexandria squeezing the seats as he rounded the soft turns in the road that led farther into the woods.

"Where is she heading?" asked Jon. "Where does this lead?"

Iris thought about it for a moment. "This road goes to the old airport. She probably intends to fly out of Glatana."

Jon swallowed hard and narrowed his determination. "Of course, she does."

Iris handed his weapons up to the front seat and patted Jon on the shoulder. "You can do this, Agent Orion."

Jon felt the roar of the engine grow louder and the pedal hit the floor. The RPM needle soared, and the transmission chugged as they drove after Ruby. Alexandria was still wounded and was going to be needing medical care sooner than later. Time was running thin.

Chapter Twelve

As the car drew nearer to Ruby's Jon tightened his grip on the steering wheel. Iris held Alexandria tightly as Jon jerked the tires and brought his front passenger fender into the rear side of Ruby's car. She corrected her direction and pulled ahead of them.

"Don't let her get away!" shouted Iris.

Jon shifted gears and pushed the car forward enough to try again. He brought the front of his car crashing into Ruby's, and she nearly drove off the road. A few other cars swerved to get out of the way as they both flew by.

"Look out!" said Iris as they narrowly avoided slamming into the back of a large truck.

Jon again got his tires in position to ram Ruby's vehicle, and this time she drove off into the grass next to an abandoned building. She came to a stop and exited the car before Jon could get turned back around and park next to her. She ran inside the building and slammed the door behind her.

"I must get in there. Will you be alright out here?" asked Jon.

"Go, Jon, go!" said Iris.

Jon grabbed the weapons from the seat and left the others behind. He approached the building with his gun at the ready. Each step slowly stretched out and carried him closer until he could press up against the siding. Some of the windows around were busted out and Jon tried to see or hear inside.

"Ruby?" he said. "Come out of there. You can't escape now."

No response came. Jon hopped the wall and through a window to get inside. Old furniture was scattered through the building and covered with dirty sheets. The smell of mold and rotting wood filled Jon's nose and he fought the urge to hold his breath.

"Come on Ruby. We don't have to play this game. Give us The Devil's Eye and turn yourself in," he said.

From a second-floor balcony a bookcase full of books came tumbling down and nearly landed on Jon. The books cascaded and some managed to catch him. He guarded his head and looked up, but Ruby wasn't there.

"That wasn't very nice," he said.

The stairs were old and some of the steps were completely caved in. Jon gripped the rail and pulled himself up to the second floor. Three doors were on the wall and one of them was hanging off the hinges. It led to the bathroom. But the other two doors were closed, so Jon stood in cover next to the door on the left.

"I'm coming in Ruby," he said. Jon's foot kicked the door wide open to reveal the bedroom within.

The bed frame held no mattress, and the old wardrobe wasn't big enough for Ruby to hide in. Jon entered the room and pondered the window, but it seemed to be impossible to pry open.

"Wrong door," said Ruby from behind Jon. She had the .22 HDM pointed at Jon's heart.

"I suppose you have me dead to rights," said Jon.

"I told you not to chase me," said Ruby. "You could have survived all of this."

Jon pushed himself against the gun and leaned in as if to kiss her. She pulled away. He smiled.

"Go ahead and pull the trigger then," said Jon.

Ruby hesitated. She looked him directly in the eyes and sighed before pulling the trigger. The gun clicked.

"What?" she said in a panic.

"You've run out of bullets," said Jon.

Ruby cocked the gun and clicked it repeatedly but to no avail. She had fired her last shot. Jon lifted his gun back up and held it on her.

"The Devil's Eye. Give it to me," he said.

Ruby's eyes widened in a craze. She dropped the gun and clutched the gem in both hands. "You'll never take it from me."

"Don't be ridiculous," said Jon. "It's over."

He stepped forward and she began scratching at his skin. Clawing for anything. He brushed her away and pulled the ruby from her hands. She collapsed to the floor and began to sob.

"My whole life. How can you take away my entire life?" she pleaded.

"You should have lived better," said Jon.

This triggered her to stand back up and quickly attempt to wrestle Iris's gun from Jon's hand. He dropped The Devil's Eye, and it bounced across the floor. Ruby let out a scream that pierced Jon's ears but continued to fight for the gun in his hands. Though hc did not wish to, he knocked her unconscious.

"I'm sorry," he whispered.

Jon picked up the gem that had caused the entire ordeal and put it in his pocket as if it were worthless. Then he tied Ruby's hands behind her back using one of the dirty sheets on the old furniture. He scooped her up and carried her back outside. Iris and Alexandria were waiting in the car.

"I thought you were a dead man," joked Iris.

But the sight of Alexandria and her blood covered bandage made Jon pause. "We need to get her somewhere fast."

Jon dumped Ruby in the empty seat and climbed back into the driver side. The car jumped to life, and he turned to Iris.

"Where's the nearest medical facility?" he asked.

Iris thought for a moment. "Get moving, I'll tell you along the way."

The drive was filled with tension as Jon waited for Ruby to awaken at any moment. Meanwhile, Alexandria was groaning in pain and barely conscious herself.

"She's losing too much blood, Jon. The bandage isn't holding," said Iris.

"I'm trying. The car only goes so fast!"

Jon rushed into the hospital with Alexandria in his arms and laid her down on the bed before they wheeled her into a room. He left Iris with Ruby unconscious in the passenger seat of the car. As the clock on the wall seemed to tick as loudly as a drum Jon waited for someone to come and tell him Alexandria's condition. Finally, a very old doctor with a thick mustache approached him.

"I have good news," he said. "She's alert, *and* she should get to keep her leg."

The old man let out a little chuckle that made Jon cringe, but he was relieved to hear it. "Can I see her?" he asked.

"Yes, go right in," said the strange doctor.

Alexandria was laid up and barely propped against a pillow. She smiled as Jon walked in. "You've gotten me into quite a lot of trouble recently. Tell me it's been worth something."

Jon sat down beside her and kissed her hand. "Arnoldo Trench has been killed. My partner and I have The Devil's Eye ruby. It's safe to say your life here will be peaceful now."

"That almost sounds boring," said Alexandria. "Especially after all this."

Her voice was frail but tender. She laughed and it made Jon smile. "Did they say how long you'll have to stay here?"

"They didn't tell me. But I'm in no hurry. I like keeping my legs," she said. They both laughed.

"I'll be heading back to Arcadia soon," said Jon. "I have to finish up and report everything to my superior."

Alexandria grew rather sad. For his part even Jon felt the sorrow. "I guess we might never see each other again," she said.

"Oh, you never know," said Jon. But he knew she was probably right.

She reached for his hand and held it tight. "You were certainly the best driver I ever hired."

They looked at each other sweetly and Jon kissed her on the cheek. "Maybe another time."

"Maybe," she said. And he left.

Iris was waiting in the car with Ruby, who had now woken back up. She sat glaring at Jon with a look that could have burnt a hole through his head.

"Have a nice nap?" he asked her.

"I will get it back. You can't keep me away from it," said Ruby.

Iris shook his head and looked at Jon as if he were crazy. "You actually like this broad?" he asked.

"Ruby?" said Jon. "No, I liked a woman named Sheena."

Ruby rocked in her seat and tried to lean toward Jon's pocket where he had stashed the gem. But Jon pushed her back away.

"They're going to put you in our best facility Ms. Windego. I hope it was worth it," he said.

She lashed out but could do nothing as Jon turned the wheel and began to drive.

As they pulled away from the hospital Jon watched as it faded behind them in the rearview mirrors. He wondered at the life Alexandria might live now that her history with Arnoldo Trench and the jewel thieves was a thing of the past. He pondered how to explain everything to the headmistress, and he tried to ignore Ruby's continued attempts to get into his pocket.

A group of officers took Ruby after they exited the plane back on Arcadian soil. She screamed and fought to get away from their grip but was muscled away. Jon and Iris walked together and were escorted down a long hallway that went to the office of the headmistress. Together they waited for her to call them inside. She sent for Iris first. Jon just waited.

"How was it?" he asked as Iris returned.

"It could have been worse. We got the job done," replied Iris.

"Yeah. *You* didn't get involved with all of the wrong women though."

Iris smiled and patted Jon on the shoulder. "I'll leave that up to you, partner. It was nice working with you."

Jon shook his hand, and they shared a moment. "We'll have to do it again sometime."

"I hope not," said Iris, but his laugh betrayed that he didn't mean it.

The two men separated, and Jon went through the giant doors that opened to the headmistress. Her giant glass desk sat opposite Jon, and she spun in her high-backed chair to look him over.

"Well, well," she said. "You really had an adventure this time, didn't you Agent Orion?"

"Yes, headmistress," said Jon. "But the job was completed, and I've brought you this."

He placed The Devil's Eye on her desk, and she looked as the midday sun beat through the window upon it. It glistened and sparkled as she cracked a grin.

"What will I do with you, Jon?" she asked.

"I'm hoping not too much," he responded. "What will you do with the jewel?"

"It will be destroyed. Broken into smaller gems and then sold. The money will be donated to charity under an anonymous name," said the headmistress.

She crossed her fingers and rested her elbows on the table. Her lips became tight, and Jon felt a small chill go down his spine.

"A wild goose chase across three different countries. Dozens of dead men and ample amounts of destroyed property. You put others' lives at risk and barely managed to escape with your own life intact." she said.

"You're right," said Jon. "I could have handled some things…differently."

"It's been quite easy to make the decision on what to do with you. Do you know what I've decided?"

"What, headmistress?" asked Jon.

She stood up and walked across the floor of her office to a file cabinet. She shuffled through some papers and withdrew some paperwork. Her slender hand laid it on the desk in front of Jon.

"What's this?" he asked.

"I've decided we're going to be changing some of our policies here at S.O.," said the headmistress.

"I don't quite understand." said Jon.

"We're going to start letting you know more about the missions we send you on. We no longer want to just send you in blindly and expect you to jump from job to job. You've pointed out how important it is that we trust our agents completely."

Jon could hardly believe his ears. He scanned over the paperwork, and it outlined the various ways that the headmistress intended to handle things differently. He shut the folder and looked up at her.

"You are to be commended, Agent Orion," she said.

"What about Iris?" asked Jon. "He was just as much a part of our success as I was."

"Of course," said the headmistress. "Both of you will be awarded honors for what you have done."

Jon shook his head in disbelief. "I can hardly believe it."

"Believe it," said the headmistress plainly. "Get over it quickly though. We have another job lined up for you immediately."

"Already?" asked Jon.

"The world never stops moving, Agent Orion," she said.

Jon agreed. Then he decided to get pushy. "Can I make a request?"

She tilted her head but conceded. "What is it?"

"May I request that I work with Agent Iris again going forward?" asked Jon.

Her eyebrows raised and she considered it. But she relented and agreed. "I will inform someone to let him know."

"Thank you," said Jon.

The headmistress pursed her lips and waved at the door. But before Jon could leave completely, she stopped him. "Oh, one more thing Jon."

"Yes, headmistress?" he asked her.

"I know that you developed a bit of a thing for that woman in Glatana. *Alexandria Leaving*. I thought you might like to know that she's doing quite well."

Jon kept silent.

"We reached out to her on your behalf," said the headmistress. "She would like to see you again."

"Is that against regulation?" asked Jon.

"Yes, which is why we're sure that you'll be trying to see her shortly," finished the headmistress, and she waved for Jon to leave.

Jon walked back out into the hall and looked up at the giant walls of S.O. headquarters. Officers and agents bustled about on various jobs, and the sounds of machines and devices humming in the distance echoed out. Jon took in a deep breath and let it flow. A man in a brown jacket approached him and Jon shook his hand.

"I suppose you'll be the one to tell me where I'm going next?" asked Jon.

"I'm told Agent Iris will be working with you again," said the man.

"Isn't that nice?" joked Jon.

The man nodded, and together they walked into another room filled with dials and maps. Iris had already been pulled aside and was waiting for them.

"You got me roped into this?" he asked Jon.

"I told them I never wanted to see your ugly face again," said Jon.

The two men smiled as the rest of the people in the room looked on impatiently.

"What do we have here anyway?" he asked them.

"Probably some fool wants to take over the world," joked Iris.

But the serious look on the other people's faces caught Jon and Iris off guard. "Wait, *really*?"

"It seems someone is trying to get their hands on some of our missing nuclear warheads," said a small man with round glasses.

"I wouldn't have it any other way," said Jon.

THE END

Visit

www.codygoggin.bandcamp.com